SHORT MYSTERY 10-PACK

MICHAEL KINGSWOOD

Contents

A mysterious stranger upsets life in a quiet bookstore.

A police negotiator finds more than he bargained for on his latest case.

A quick trip to the liquor store becomes exciting. And dangerous.

Private Investigators seek to recover a lost heirloom.

A man goes hunting for more than game.

A dog on a run with his best buddy makes a grim discovery.

A simple courier job turns deadly.

Fresh out of prison, a man seeks revenge on the woman who framed him.

A client's cryptic story leads Private Investigators to evidence of multiple murders.

A bag of money makes a day at the beach very interesting.

A collection of 10 short mysteries from author Michael Kingswood, Short Mystery 10-Pack contains the stories Popper's, Across The Line, Abe's Liquors, The Billionaire's Daughter, Hunting For Game, Give A Dog A Bone, Bag Man, Fresh Out, The Suspect's Wife, and Beach Bags.

Enjoy the book! After you're done, please come to Michael's website and sign up for his mailing list at michaelkingswood.com/newsletter-signup/. Guaranteed to be spam free, he uses it to announce new releases and special promotions for his fans.

Popper's

A Short Mystery

Michael Kingswood

Popper's

New customers come through Popper's bookstore all the time. But one of them, an average man in every way, has David very concerned that he intends more than just buying books.

I t was nearing the end of David's shift at Popper's Books And Things. Even for a Tuesday, it had been a slow day. Maybe half a dozen people had actually bought something all day; not for the first time, he pondered whether working the counter at a small bookstore was the best summer job for him to have taken.

He was an Engineering major, not in the liberal arts. He probably should have pushed to find something more related to his field.

But he couldn't even apply for a summer intern position until after the end of next school year, and there was something about Popper's...

He'd discovered it his second week at school, and before long it had become the place he hung out in more than any other.

The antique but carefully preserved and polished mahogany counter running half the length of the store to the right of the entrance, where the staff kept watch over the customers like a bartender looking out over his pub.

The six rows of equally-polished hardwood shelves—not mahogany but still nice—that took up the center of the shop's space.

The wall shelves to the left of the entrance that housed new release comics of every variety, and the backlist boxes at the rear.

The small brown leather couch against the wall past the end of the counter, and the two matching stuffed chairs opposite it where customers could read or sip a cup from the pot that Barbara, the owner, insisted be maintained freshly-brewed and available at all times.

And, of course, the game room in back, complete with all the miniatures a game master and his groups of players could need for the evening, an old and battered but still running refrigerator where the players could stash snacks and—nonalcoholic—drinks, and a trio of tables sized for eight so that there was almost always room to get a game on.

Barbara kept the shelves well-stocked with a mix of new and used tomes, and liked to spray the place down with a different air freshener each week. Today, that meant the place had the mixed odor of french roast and lavender, with just a hint of old paper beneath.

Add the light jazz that made up the shop's approved playlist, piped from the cashier's iMac to bluetooth speakers nestled at each corner of the shop's main room, and it was a nice, homey, welcoming place.

Just lacking in customers. Today, at least.

David had the register app open on the iMac and was just getting started reconciling the take for his shift—not a hard task today—when the little bell mounted above the entrance rang.

A customer.

He looked up, and his hackles rose immediately.

The guy was average looking. As average as it was possible to be: height, build, facial features, hair…all the way down to his beige suit. He would have had to work to be more unno-ticeable.

Except that as he approached David's counter, doffing the sunglasses he had been wearing to reveal light brown eyes, he gave off a sense of presence, of power right on the edge of control, and David knew this was no ordinary, average guy, however he may look.

"Can I help you?"

The guy folded up his shades and slipped them into the inner pocket of his suit coat. He remained silent for a couple seconds, and glanced to his left, toward the gaming room. Checking to see if anyone was back there?

Finally, the man looked back at David, and the intensity of that very average stare made him want to shift on his feet.

"I don't know, David. Can you help me?"

David swallowed. "How do you know my name?"

The man's lips turned upward into the smallest hint of a smile. "Store's website," he said, and David felt heat rise to his cheeks in embarrassment.

He'd forgotten about the staff pictures Barbara posted there; it had seemed silly to put him up since he was just around for the summer, but she'd insisted.

The man let a few seconds pass in silence, then made a little shrug and looked toward the back room again. "Is Barbara here?"

"No, she's coming in for the evening shift today. Should be here in twenty minutes or so."

"Ah." He nodded as though David had said something profound.

"There's coffee if you want to wait for her."

"No, I must be off. Just tell her Henry said hello, and I look forward to catching up with her soon."

Then he turned and walked out. David couldn't help thinking the plain name suited his plainness perfectly.

It made him distinctly uneasy.

By the time Barbara showed up—thirty minutes later—he still had not been able to put the guy out of his mind. Something was just…off…about him, and the whole situation there.

Barbara was all smiles, as usual, as she walked in the door. She had her reddish-brown hair up, her curls mostly bundled away in an intricate mass of braids and twists and what-have-yous that was impossible to follow, and wore jeans and a loose green collared blouse. In her mid 30s, she was a bit on the plump side, but what she lacked in sexiness she made up for in good old fashioned fun personality.

"Hey David," she said, as she swept through the door and over to the counter. "Good day?"

He shrugged. "Slow day."

"Well, it's Tuesday," she said, and maneuvered down toward the coffee pot over next to the couch.

"Yeah." David logged out of the register app and picked up his backpack, from where he had left it in the corner behind the counter. "Accounts are all square."

Barbara nodded, not taking her eyes away from the cup she was pouring. "Ok, thanks. Have a great night."

"You too." David slipped out from behind the counter, maneuvering carefully to avoid bumping into her as he passed her by. "By the way," he said as he started toward the door, "your friend Henry stopped by to say hi."

"What?"

The sudden change in her tone made him turn back to look at her, concern rising within him. She sounded like she really hoped she had heard him wrong.

"Henry. Plain guy. Really average, but…also not? He said hi, and that he wants to see you again soon."

Her hand that was holding the cup began to shake, and then the coffee she was pouring into the cup ran over.

Barbara made a yelp of pain and chagrin as the scalding liquid spilled over onto her hand. She reflexively shook the hand, flinging the coffee off, but lost her grip on the cup.

It fell and shattered on the false-wood laminate floor, coffee spilling all over the place.

"Damn!" Barbara said, and raised her burned hand to her mouth.

"Are you ok?" David said, rushing toward her.

She put the pot back down and waved him away. "I'm fine. I'm fine. Just…you surprised me."

"Let me help clean up."

"No. No, you go. You're seeing Lindsay again tonight right?" She put on a smile, but David could tell it was forced. "Don't want to be late."

No. No, he really didn't. Lindsay was something else. But…

"You sure you're alright?" He glanced toward the door, recalling the look on Henry's face when he'd been there earlier. "Who is that guy?"

"Just…a friend. An old friend."

"Boyfriend?" He tried to make his tone light, but failed and he knew it.

Barbara shrugged. "The one that got away. Kind of?" Again with the smile that really wasn't. "Go on, get out of here."

David hesitated, and she made a shooing gesture. "Go!"

He went.

***

DAVID HAD the evening shift Thursday. When he came into the Popper's, Henry was there, with Barbara.

Henry had on the same beige suit as before, and stood in front of the counter in the same casual, yet also not, pose that he had used before.

Barbara was behind the counter, in her red and white stripped shirt and wearing a not happy expression.

When the bell over the door rang, announcing David's presence, both of them turned to look his way.

Barbara immediately tried—and failed—to put a relaxed smile on her face.

Henry gave David a once-over, then sniffed ever so softly. He looked back at Barbara and said, "Three days. Think about it."

Then he turned away from the counter and walked out. "David," Henry said as he walked past. It was both greeting and dismissal. And then he was gone.

David watched the door close behind him, then looked back at Barbara, both eyebrows raising.

Barbara met his gaze for a second, then looked away

toward the iMac screen. "It's been a busy day," she said, and began typing away at the keyboard. "But I've got the accounts register up to date. There are two groups in the back."

David nodded, though she couldn't see, and moved over to the counter. "What was going on there?"

Barbara's lips compressed. She continued typing, but didn't reply.

"Barbara - "

"It's not your concern," she snapped, and David flinched.

She had never raised her voice like that, to anyone. Not in most of the year that he had been coming here, and that he had known her.

Barbara seemed to realize she had crossed a line. She stopped typing and just looked at the screen for a few seconds. Then, with a sigh, she turned her eyes back onto David.

"I appreciate you're worried, but you don't need to be. It's just some old business Henry and I have to resolve. I'm a big girl; I can handle it." She grinned mischievously then, and added, "And you have better things to be thinking about. You never told me how it went with Lindsay the other night."

It was a painfully obvious change in subject. She didn't want him involved with whatever was going on between her and David, that much was clear.

And, he reminded himself, she was almost twice his age. Pretty sure she knew how to handle herself.

So he went with the change in subject.

This time.

HENRY DIDN'T COME AROUND AGAIN that David saw, but the effects of his presence lingered. Barbara seemed distracted, and on-edge, as the work-week ended and the weekend began.

Normally David would not work the weekend. Barbara had

a couple part-timers who handled the counter on Saturdays and Sundays, and though Popper's was open late on Saturday she closed up early on Sundays, so there really wasn't any need for him.

But he found himself in the shop more often than not most weekends anyway. His D&D group met there Saturday afternoons, and a lot of the time there was a writer on a signing tour or something else cool going on so he ended up sticking around after the game.

This weekend, he decided he was going to keep as close an eye on the shop—and Barbara—as he could. Henry had said something was going down in three days. That meant Sunday. And though Barbara's assurance that there wasn't a problem stymied David's initial suspicions, her continued obvious discomfort made him determined to help.

If he could.

So he stayed late after his D&D game, until closing time. Lindsay wanted to hook up that night, but he begged off, honestly saying a friend needed his help.

Still, as he sat on the couch in Popper's and read the latest Grisham book while Henry steadfastly didn't come into the shop and Barbara had absolutely no difficulty at all all night, David wondered what the hell he thought he was doing.

* * *

SUNDAY DAWNED BRIGHT AND SUNNY, and David went out for his morning run.

While he was making his way through mile 3, he let his thoughts go, and he really considered what was going on. What he was doing.

Henry and Barbara had a previous relationship.

Something about Henry himself had certainly made David uncomfortable.

But maybe he was just projecting his own crap onto Barbara. She had seemed uncomfortable when he first mentioned Henry to her, but that was attributable to hearing from an old acquaintance after a long hiatus.

And David had no idea what he had stepped into when he arrived for work the other day. For all he knew, Henry had been trying to ask her out, and she felt embarrassed because David had walked in, not because of anything Henry had done.

She certainly didn't want to talk to David about it; but then she didn't really have to, did she? They were friendly, but she wasn't his friend. She was his boss, and quite a bit older than he was.

By the time he got home after his Sunday 5 miles, he convinced himself that he was just being silly.

And he had passed up a good, hot time with Lindsay last night, for nothing.

Dumbass.

He resolutely did not go to the shop. Instead, he met up with some friends for lunch.

He was just saying goodbye to them and heading for the bus stop to ride over to Lindsay's place when his cell phone rang. He looked at the screen. It was Popper's.

"Hello?"

"David, it's Sonya." Sonya was the part-timer who handled Sundays. "Have you heard from Barbara?"

He frowned and looked at the time. Almost three o'clock. "No, why?"

"Well, she usually comes by before closeup to check on things, but I haven't seen her. Did she tell you anything about it? I've never closed by myself. Should I just lock the door, or… ? But I don't have a key!"

"Have you tried calling her?"

"Yeah, it goes straight to voicemail."

David's frown grew, and a shiver went down his spine. This was completely unlike Barbara, and he immediately flashed to that brief interchange between her and Henry.

Three days. Think about it.

What had that guy done?

"David?"

He blinked, and came back to present. Sonya had been talking, but he had not heard a thing she'd said. Didn't matter, though.

"There's a spare key in the top drawer of the desk in the office behind the game room. Just shut down the computer, turn off the lights, and lock up. I've got the early shift tomorrow. You can bring the key back then."

"You sure? Ok, thanks."

She hung up.

David immediately tried calling Barbara himself.

Voicemail.

He swore under his breath. His mind raced, and he tried to think of what to do.

Call the cops?

And tell them what, that a grown woman hadn't returned a call? They'd tell him to take a hike.

He had Barbara's address with her contact information in his phone. He looked at it, uncertain.

Maybe she was just running late, and Sonya was being flighty. Or maybe she and Henry had hooked up, for real.

Or maybe he was doing something horrible to her, that David would hear about tomorrow on the breaking news.

Screw it.

He opened up his Uber app.

DAVID HAD BEEN to Barbara's house once before, for an end-of-the-school-year party she'd thrown for her employees and friends of the store. It was a nicely maintained two bedroom bungalow on the north side of town, maybe a thousand square feet. Yellow siding with white trim, a porch the length of the house in front, a shingle roof, and a carport on a triangular lot that was stuck between two slightly-larger houses that were obviously by the same builder.

She had a stylized mailbox post that was carved in mermaids, and a mermaid-emblazoned welcome mat on her front porch. The lawn was closely trimmed, and she had chest-high screening bushes on either side of her lot. And that was it. No frills.

When David got out of the Uber, he saw that her car was in the driveway and her front door was slightly ajar. That wasn't necessarily an indication of trouble if she was home, but still, that anxious feeling that had been growing in his stomach since Sonya's call grew more intense.

He hurried up the walk from the street to the front door and stopped, listening.

A man's voice—he was sure it was Henry's—came through the crack between the door and the jamb. He sounded angry, but the voice was muffled so David couldn't make out what he was saying.

Adrenalin kicked in. Hard.

David slowly pushed the door open and fished his phone out.

The front sitting room was empty. David stepped inside and moved to the hallway that led back to the kitchen. There was a light on back there. Inching forward down the hall, he could hear Henry more clearly now.

" - not good enough, you dumb bitch."

Oh yeah. This wasn't good at all.

David called 911. The operator picked up, and he whispered, "There's an intruder in my friend's house." He gave the address.

The operator asked a question, but the sound of shattering glass from back in the kitchen overwhelmed David's hearing.

Before he could think about what he was doing, he surged forward and stepped into the kitchen.

Barbara was there, dressed in jeans and a white t-shirt. She was backed up against the wall opposite the doorway David had walked in through.

Henry was in front of her, his back to David. Again he had the beige suit on.

The glass David had heard breaking was lying at the base of the wall to Barbara's right, a jumbled pile of shards. Streaks of water flowed down the wall above the pile; Henry must have thrown the glass at the wall and it shattered there.

"There's nothing else, Henry," Barbara was saying as David stepped inside. "If you - " She saw him and her words cut off in a choking sound as her eyes went wide.

Henry noticed her change in demeanor. He made a quarter-turn to his left and looked behind himself. Seeing David there, his eyebrow rose.

"David. Nice to see you again." He no longer had the calm certitude he'd had the last couple times David had seen him, but the feeling of power was still there. It just was no longer in check. "Who you on the phone with?"

Only then did David realize he still had the phone up to his left ear, and that the 911 operator was talking.

"The cops," David said.

Henry made a tsking sound and shook his head. "Real sorry to hear that, kid."

He turned fully toward David and raised his right hand.

David saw the gun coming up to point at him, and everything seemed to slow to a crawl.

He wasn't old enough to get a carry permit yet, but his dad had spent a lot of time teaching him to shoot. One by one, his brain clicked past the rules of gun safety, as Henry violated them.

Treat every gun as if it's loaded. Ok, not really a violation, but…

Don't point the gun at anything you're not willing to shoot. Clear violation here.

Keep your finger off the trigger until you're ready to shoot.

Henry's trigger finger left its position along the slide of his pistol and slipped inside the trigger guard.

Oh crap, he *hadn't* violated rule number two, because he clearly was more than willing to shoot!

Duck!

The sound of a pistol shot turned time back to normal speed, but David didn't feel anything hit him, and Henry was close enough there was no way he could have missed.

Henry's arm dipped, and his expression became confused. He half-turned back toward Barbara, and a trickle of blood ran from the corner of his mouth.

"Barb- " he started to say.

She shot again. Henry's head jerked, and he collapsed to the floor.

David and Barbara stared at each other from across the room.

Her shirt was untucked on her right side, where she must have pulled it out to get at her concealed holster. The little pistol in her hands looked huge right then, and residual gunsmoke curled up from the end of its barrel.

She lowered the weapon to her side and said something, but David didn't actually hear it.

All he could hear was the pounding of his heart, the highly concerned babbling of the 911 operator, and, far away but getting closer by the second, the wailing of police sirens.

It took hours for the cops to get done with him. When he'd finally finished giving his statement and being interviewed, and interviewed, and re-interviewed, it was late and he wanted nothing but to go to bed.

He'd called his buddy Steve to come pick him up from the police station—an Uber didn't really seem like the thing right then—but Steve hadn't arrived yet, so he sat down on a bench in the public waiting section of the station.

He'd been sitting there for about five minutes when the door leading back into the innards of the station opened and Barbara walked out.

She looked just as beat as David felt, and she made a beeline toward the exit. But when she saw him, she stopped and walked over to the bench where he was sitting.

He watched her come, feeling numb and uncertain about everything. When she gestured toward the seat next to him, he just shrugged and she sat.

"I owe you an explanation," she said.

"That would be nice."

Barbara looked down a drew a breath. "When I was about your age, I got married. His name was Henry Popper." She looked back up into his eyes and raised an eyebrow.

David saw the import of the name immediately.

"He was everything you saw and more - dashing, exciting…and a criminal. I knew he was, but I didn't care. That was part of what made him so exciting and sexy. Well, he made this big heist, got a lot of money. And he got caught." Barbara shook her head. "After he went to prison I saw where my life would end up if I stuck with him. So I got a divorce."

"He went through all this because he was sore at you for dumping him?"

She shook her head. "The cops never found all the money

he stole. But I knew where it was. I took it, changed my name, and moved away. I traveled for a while, and eventually ended up here. Used the money to buy a place and open my shop. Named it after him, for sentimental reasons I guess. Or maybe just stupidity. Regardless, after all this time I thought I'd covered my tracks, but…" She spread her hands.

"So he wanted his money back."

Barbara nodded. "With interest. But of course, the money was gone. Most of it. Into the house and the business. I thought…hoped…he'd accept a cut of the profits, let me pay him back over time. But…well, he was never as smart as he made on."

David nodded. It all made sense. But… "Are you going to be in trouble?"

Barbara looked askance at him. "No, of course not. It was a home invasion. I have a carry permit, but even if I didn't, he assaulted both of us with deadly force in my home. Totally justified shooting, morally and legally."

David had assumed that was the case from the beginning. "I meant about the money."

"Oh." She considered for a few seconds, then shrugged. "Statute of limitations for the heists he pulled are well past."

"Well, that's good I guess."

Barbara put her hand atop David's and gave his a little squeeze. "I'm sorry you had to go through that, David. More sorry than I can tell you."

"Yeah. Well, I - " David's phone buzzed, cutting him off.

He looked down and saw a text from Steve. He was out front.

David removed his hand from Barbara's and stood. "My ride's here. I gotta go."

Barbara's expression was unreadable. "Will I see you back at the shop, or - ?"

"I don't know. I need to think things through."

"I understand."

David nodded, then turned toward the exit. He stopped after half a dozen steps and turned back around to face her.

"Thanks for not letting him shoot me.'

Barbara smiled, a sad little smile that said she feared their friendship was at an end. "You're welcome."

Then David walked out of the Police Station. He needed to rest, and think. And decide whether he would go back to the store that bore the name of the man Barbara had killed.

Or not.

Across The Line

Duty Only Goes So Far

Michael Kingswood

Author of The Davidson & Harper Mysteries

Across The Line

Bentonville Police Department's top hostage negotiator has seen it all, but even still nothing could prepare him for what he finds when he rolls into a seemingly routine convenience store holdup.

A nother nutcase.

It never failed. Every time it looked like Sergeant Cole's Friday was going to be quiet, some joker decided to rob a bank, take hostages in an office building, or do something stupid like that. The perp was almost never seriously interested in hurting anyone, of course. Most times, the hostages were a result of his half-assed plan falling apart, and Cole was able to talk him down without too much trouble.

So when he got the call of shots fired and hostages taken at a Convenience Store at the corner of State Street and Cunningham Boulevard, Cole just rolled his eyes in annoyance.

Really, a Convenience Store? The jackass couldn't at least hit a place that would make it worth all the trouble and effort?

Perps tended to be stupid, otherwise they'd be working as Engineers or something. But still, this sort of caper always made Cole wonder how the perp managed to take a bath without drowning.

Cole took his time, refilling his coffee thermos and hitting the bathroom before donning his blue Bentonville PD jacket over his white polo shirt and khakis. Then he strapped on his sidearm and left the precinct station.

All things considered, it was a beautiful summer day. A few puffy clouds moved slowly across the sky, pushed by a gentle breeze. Though it was already quite warm, the humidity was lower than it had been.

A good day for fishing, but there was no way Cole would be able to cut out early now.

The drive from the precinct to the scene would have been quick even without his siren and lights; it was only about two miles away. All the same, by the time he pulled up, the store was ringed with police cruisers. There were probably twenty cops crouching behind the cars, guns drawn. Looking to the right, Cole wasn't surprised to see a sniper team setting up atop the strip mall across the street.

They probably wouldn't be needed, of course. It almost never came to that.

Putting his cruiser into park, Cole opened the door and got out. He had to maneuver a little bit to get his belly around the steering wheel, a reminder that he really needed to start exercising again, and go back on Weight Watchers.

Muttering to himself, Cole shut the door and walked over to the command station. There, he got a surprise.

The scene commander was Bill Kennedy, dressed as always in a well-pressed Navy-blue business suit with an unobtrusive tie. Bill always looked more like a banker than a cop, but he was shrewd and tough. Cole had come up through the Academy with Bill, and was Godfather to one of his kids. They didn't get to interact very much professionally these days, though, since Bill got promoted and sent to a job in Narcotics.

Why was he here, for a robbery case?

"Hi Bill," said Cole as he walked up.

"Good to see you, Greg," Bill replied, shaking his hand quickly with a firm grip

At Bill's side was Helen Duval, head of the Robbery/Homicide unit. She always looked good, and today was no different. She was sporting a tight-fitting pair of bluejeans and a Bentonville PD polo shirt, very similar to Cole's own, and had her brown hair done up in a bun on the back of her head. Once upon a time, Greg had a thing for her, but that was before he got married and was ruined for women forever. She was busy talking with two uniformed officers, but nodded in greeting to Cole in between issuing orders.

"What brings Narcotics out here, Bill?"

"I've got an undercover in there with the perps. They were supposed to be on their way to a deal, but one of the perps freaked out or something, and it all went to hell."

Cole winced. That was a tough spot. He'd never even considered putting his name in for undercover work, but he respected the hell out of the guys who did. Cole couldn't imagine how those guys did it, day in day out, without losing themselves in the criminal world. Truth be told, some did cross the line, but it was a very small minority, much fewer than Cole would have thought.

"I guess we'll have to be extra careful on this one then," he said. "Let's have a look."

He and Bill left the command post and moved up to the ring of cruisers. As they crouched down behind one of the car hoods for cover, Bill handed him a pair of binoculars. Peering through, he could barely make out details inside the store through the tinted windows. Shelves of items for sale, a few signs…nothing really stood out. Wait. He saw some movement, a shadowy figure walking down one of the aisles.

"Ok, I think I see one of the perps. Any idea where the hostages are?"

Bill shook his head, but before he could speak Helen joined them, interjecting.

"We haven't made contact yet, Sergeant, but we'll have the phone hooked up in a minute. We'll use the normal protocol, I assume?"

"I don't see why not…"

Cole froze. As he was lowering the binoculars, he noticed one of the cars parked in front of the store: a red Ford Focus. Oh no… Raising the binoculars back up to his eyes, he read the license plate, and his heart sank. "Oh my God."

He could feel Helen and Bill's eyes boring into him, though he didn't take his eyes away from the eyepieces.

"What, Greg? What's wrong?"

Cole could hear the tension in Bill's voice, matching the sudden fright he felt himself. He realized he was shaking, and lowered the binoculars. "That's my son's car," Cole said, and was surprised to hear his voice quavering.

Bill breathed a curse. "Can you do this, Greg? We can get someone else."

Cole snorted. "Who, Webster? He couldn't find his ass with two hands. No, I can handle it. I hope."

Looking back at them, Cole could see the doubt in both Bill and Helen's eyes. Particularly Helen's. The two of them exchanged a look, then Helen said, "How about we call him in anyway, just in case."

Righteous indignation flooded Cole in a rush. Where did they get off second-guessing him? He was the best negotiator on the force, and…and he was forced to admit that they were right to be concerned. His thoughts kept going back to Jeffrey, all of seventeen years old, no doubt terrified by what was going on inside the store. Reluctantly, Cole nodded.

"Ok, call him in. But he's here in an assisting role only, agreed?"

Both of them nodded.

"Now where's that phone?"

The three of them straightened and walked back to the command van. As they arrived, technicians were just finishing hooking up the portable telephone equipment. One of the technicians nodded to Cole and handed him the receiver. "Should be coming online now," the tech said. Sure enough, a dial tone issued from earpiece. It only took a moment to get the number to the phone inside the store, then Cole dialed it in and waited.

No one picked up after five rings, but Cole didn't hang up. As he listened to the ring tones continuing, he imagined what was going on inside. The perps debating amongst themselves whether to answer or not. The hostages, his son, cowering in the back corner fearing what the perps would do next. The perps, becoming annoyed with the ringing, beginning to argue more heatedly until they finally dared one of their group to pick up the phone…

Right on cue, someone answered.

"Who is this?" asked a gruff, but young, male voice.

"This is Sergeant Gregory Cole of the Bentonville Police Department. Who am I speaking to?"

"Carl."

"Ok Carl, how is everyone in there?"

"How do you think, Sergeant Cole? We - "

In the background, Cole heard another voice speaking. "Oh shit, that's my - "

"Jeff, shut the fuck up," said Carl, though his voice was muffled as though he was halfway covering the mouthpiece with his hand. But that was all Cole needed to hear. He'd know that voice anywhere. Cole's blood went like ice water, and he almost dropped the phone. Somehow, he didn't know how, he maintained his composure and managed a professional tone.

"Carl, put Jeff on the line."

There was a long pause. Cole could hear the wheels turning in the perp's head. In his mind's eye, Cole could picture Carl, whoever he was, and Jeffrey trading looks. Jeffrey shaking his head, wanting nothing more than to avoid talking with his father through that phone line. Carl licking his lips as hope that maybe an inside connection could get them out of this bloomed in his mind.

Finally, Cole heard Carl say softly, "He wants to talk to you." Then a moment later, his son's voice spoke to him over the phone.

"Dad?"

"Yeah Jeff, it's me. What the hell's going on? What are you doing mixed up in this?"

He could feel Bill and Helen's gazes again. Glancing to the side, Cole saw their expressions: Bill looking stricken, Helen looking resigned but determined. They could both hear the conversation over the speakers attached to the phone line.

Jeffrey's voice was strained. It sounded like he was barely holding back tears. "Sorry, dad. Scott and me just wanted some pot for the party tomorrow. But things got nuts, and…"

There was a moment of scuffling around on the other end of the line, then the sound of muffled voices conversing. No doubt Carl and the others didn't like that Jeffrey had revealed that much, and were trying to silence him. Finally, Jeffrey came back on the line.

"Listen, Dad - "

"No, you listen, son. I've told you how these things work. You guys are in a no-win situation here. You need to just come out and give up before someone gets hurt."

"Can't do that."

"Jeffrey…"

"No. Tell the cops to pull back. We'll get in my car and drive away. No one gets hurt, and we all go our separate ways."

The phone went dead.

"Son of a bitch," Cole breathed. For once, he knew he was telling the truth when he said that, considering his ex-wife was Jeffrey's mother.

Bill clapped him on the shoulder. "Greg, Webster will be here in a minute. You need to get off this case right now." Beside him, Helen was nodding in agreement.

Cole shook his head.

"I mean it, Greg. You can't do a negotiation with your own son and you know it."

Cole ground his teeth, the fear for Jeff's safety combined with anger at Bill's words causing the telltale ache in his belly that presaged a flareup of acid reflux. Problem was, Bill was right. Deny it all he wanted, there was no way Cole could go about this case dispassionately. If he stayed on there was a good chance folks, maybe Jeff, would get hurt or worse.

Slowly, reluctantly, Cole nodded and set the phone down. He took a step back and found himself on the ground before he even realized his legs had given out on him.

Bill and Helen were down with him in a heartbeat, concern written deeply on their faces. "You ok, Greg?" Bill asked.

Cole nodded, holding back a wince as his reflux began kicking in big-time. "Tell Webster to hurry his ass up."

<hr>

IT TOOK Webster an eternity to get to the scene.

Or at least it felt like an eternity to Cole. He managed to get back to his feet long enough to maneuver into one of the folding chairs that were set up in the command post. Then he downed some Pepto from the bottle he kept in his briefcase and settled down to wait.

The uniformed cops were fully settled into position, their ring around the store complete, by the time Webster arrived, looking disheveled. He had apparently been on the other side of town dealing with a domestic disturbance gone bad. That accounted for his delay in getting here.

Any other day, Cole would have understood completely. But today…

Webster walked up, his ugly green tie clashing with the blue Bentonville PD jacket he habitually wore. That did nothing to make Cole feel any better. If Webster couldn't even tell what kind of tie to wear with what - hell if he hadn't had the good sense to marry a woman who would talk him down from that ledge rather than push him further out onto it - he really did not have the sense to run a scene like this. Not with Cole's son wrapped up in the middle of it.

To his credit though, Webster looked genuinely concerned as he approached. "Jesus, Greg, you must feel like hell," he said. "Don't worry; we'll get Jeff out of there safe and sound."

Cole bit back a sarcastic retort and stood up, shaking Webster's hand. At least the guy had a good grip.

"Thanks, Sam," Cole said, and was surprised to find that he meant it. Webster might not be the sharpest knife in the drawer, but Cole was forced to admit he meant well and always tried, even when he fucked things up. And right then, he was the best option for Jeff's safety.

Webster smiled encouragingly and turned toward where Bill and Helen waited by the phone. The three gathered in a huddle for a few minutes. Their words did not carry to Cole's ears.

He found himself scowling. They were keeping him out of the loop, and it galled. It was also the right call. He was not a cop, not right now. He was a concerned family member of one of the host- Cole caught himself mid-thought and scowled even deeper. He was the concerned family member of one of the perps.

His own son. A fucking perp.

How had Jeff gone so wrong? How had Cole let it happen?

Or had he *made* it happen somehow?

Cole sank back in his chair and looked away from his colleagues. Staring at nothing, he let his thoughts wander back through the months and years past, trying to figure out what he had done that had helped set his son down the wrong path.

He thought of Margaret, Jeff's mother. Cast-iron bitch, almost from the beginning. Or at least once she had her claws dug into Cole good and deep. And then once she had enough years of marriage to get a cut of his pension, she vanished on him. On them. Cole heard she was banging some card player in Vegas these days, but he had no idea if that was true.

He wanted to say he didn't care, but it still stung. In spite of the God-awful way she had treated him for the last ten years or so, somewhere inside she was still the girl Cole had fallen for.

It must have been worse for Jeff. Cole had seen all the signs:

Jeff had drawn in on himself, his grades had fallen, he got into fights at school. But after a year or so, he had come back around, and Cole thought he was, if not over it at least adjusted to it, accepting their new situation. In the two years since, things had gotten better and it looked like everything between the two of them, at least, was back to normal and the future bright.

Apparently not.

Maybe if Margaret had not left. If Cole had not driven her off...

He snorted out a bitter half-laugh. If anything, she had tried to drive *him* off, if truth be told. She was only interested in one thing, and once she got it...

"Ah crap," Cole muttered.

Someone was going to have to tell Margaret what was going on with Jeff. That was not going to be a fun phone call.

With a sigh, Cole dug his cell phone out of the inner pocket of his jacket then walked away from the command station for some privacy. He had Margaret's mother's phone number still - kids still like grandma even if Mom is a bitch. She might know how to get in touch with her wayward daughter.

This was not going to be a fun call at all.

Turns out, it was even worse than Cole thought it would be.

⁕

WHEN COLE finally returned to the command station, he felt like he'd been whipped up one side and back down the other. Bill noticed immediately and raised an eyebrow at him, questioning.

"I talked to Margaret," Cole said.

"Ah."

There was nothing else to say about it, so Cole did not. Bill didn't press the issue. Bless him.

"What's the status in there?"

Bill frowned and turned his gaze on the store. "Haven't heard from them in a while, but Webster thinks they're starting to lose resolve."

"What do you think?"

Bill cleared his throat and glanced at Webster, who was talking with Helen down by the ring of cruisers in front of the store. His frown got deeper. Cole's heart sank.

His expression must have given him away, because Bill spoke quickly. "Doesn't matter what I think, Greg. You need to remain positive." He took a breath and smiled. It was the carefully practiced, false, smile that Greg had seen, and used himself, dozens of times when the situation was dire and you didn't want to panic a family member. "Everything will be fine, Greg," he said. "Honest."

Cole returned the smile in kind. "Ok. Thanks, buddy."

For a moment, he indulged in the fantasy that either of them believed a word of it. The moment did not last.

A shot rang out.

At first Cole thought one of the uniformed cops had screwed up, discharged his weapon by accident. Or at least he wanted to think that; hoped for it. But that moment passed quickly. The shot had come from the convenience store.

All around, cops pulled their weapons and took cover behind their cruisers, watching the store with rapt attention.

Nothing happened for several eternal seconds. Then the front door of the convenience store swung open and a figure stumbled out.

It was getting on toward evening; the sun was low on the horizon, casting long shadows from the nearby buildings, and the convenience store faced east. So at first it was hard to make out anything from the person except that it looked male and he was bent over, clutching at his belly with both hands as he stumbled forward several steps toward the ring of police cruisers.

Then he fell to the ground face-first.

He cried out, a long low groan of pain and fear that carried across the intervening space clearly, and Cole could see he was trying to crawl toward the cops, but he did not make fast progress.

Cole got a better look at the man's clothing, jeans and a green short-sleeved collared shirt, sneakers. It reminded him of the sort of thing Jeff wore…

Oh no.

Oh dear Lord no.

Cole looked closer. The sandy-colored hair, hanging loose to shoulder length. That green shirt…wasn't it the one Cole's mother had given him for his birthday?

No, it couldn't be.

Then he heard the moan, louder this time. More clear.

"Dad."

COLE WAS across the parking lot in a flash, heedless of the shouts from his fellow officers, and crouched down next to his son. He was aware of tears running down his cheeks, but it he paid them no mind. His only focus was on Jeff, the boy he'd held as a baby, the kid he'd played baseball with, the young man he was proud to send off to the prom.

And now the victim of a gunshot wound to the gut, bleeding out on the pavement in front of a convenience store.

All because some pissants wanted to go get stoned.

Cole helped his son roll over onto his back. He knew you weren't supposed to move an injured person but… He couldn't just leave him face-down in the street. As the wound came into view, Cole felt his breath catch in his throat. Jeff's belly was ripped open almost someone had taken a sword to it. The shot must have grazed him instead of hitting him straight-on. It must have been a larger caliber bullet, though; Cole thought he could see some of Jeff's guts trying to come out.

Terror, couple with rage, swept through him. Which was the stronger? Did it matter? They fought within Cole's soul, tearing at each other in their quest to devour him. His head whirled and he could not see for a moment.

And then all he felt was cold.

Jeff clutched at his arm with one hand - he needed the other to hold his guts in. His eyes were terrified, pleading, remorseful. "Dad, I'm sorry."

Cole said something. He wasn't sure what, but it seemed to do the trick. Jeff slumped back onto the ground, some of the guilt fading from his eyes. And did he manage a smile? No, that was a trick of the eye. Shot people don't smile.

Then he went still.

Cole heard a guttural roar, the kind of cry a beast makes. It took a moment for him to realize the roar was coming from his own mouth. He moved more quickly than he ever thought he could have, getting to his feet and rushing the convenience store door.

He had his sidearm in his hands, but had no memory of drawing it.

Somewhere in the background, people were shouting his name, ordering him to stop. It was like so many buzzing flies, just noise.

Then he was through the door.

He swept the store over the sights of his gun. A huddled cluster of people in the back corner. The hostages. A trio of men standing in a circle in front of the cooler section. They were shouting at each other. One of them held a semi-automatic handgun in his hand. Cole thought he could still see smoke rising from the muzzle.

The three men turned as one, shocked surprise on their faces.

The gunman's eyes widened and he began to raise the weapon. Cole didn't realize he had fired until the man's - the boy's really - head kicked back and the cooler behind him became splattered with blood and brain matter.

Cole turned his gun on the second man, a spindly little guy of maybe sixteen. Cole thought he might have recognized him from Jeff's school at some point.

The kid looked terrified. Cole shot him without a second thought.

Only one perp remained. He had his hands up. There was something in his left hand that flashed gold.

"I'm a cop!" he shouted, waving his left hand around frantically.

"You let them kill my son," Cole said.

Then he pulled the trigger.

COLE SAT in the back of a police cruiser, his hands cuffed behind his back. His thoughts were awhirl. The entire incident was surreal, like he had witnessed it through someone else's eyes.

But it was real. He had done it.

The white-hot rage, the coldness, had faded, leaving Cole only with the disbelief over what he had done. The guilt, threatening to crush his soul.

The satisfaction.

The passenger side front door opened and Bill climbed into the car. He sat in the seat, silently, for a long minute or so. Cole could see from his profile that he was working his jaw the way he did when he could not decide whether he was pissed or scared or what.

Cole could relate.

Finally Bill turned around and Cole was surprised to see tears in his friend's eyes. "Jesus, Greg."

Cole shrugged his shoulders, as much as he could with his hands cuffed as they were. What did Bill expect him to say, that he was sorry? He knew he should be, but he wasn't. Not really.

They sat in silence for a while, just looking at each other. The silence spoke volumes.

Then Bill inhaled quickly through his nose and wiped his eyes. "Paramedics finished up with Jeff."

Cole nodded. It hadn't taken them long; but then how much time does it take to give aid to a dead person?

"He's going to be ok, Greg."

Wait. What? Cole felt his jaw drop open. What had Bill said? Against his better judgment, Cole felt hope blossom within him. Was it possible? No. He had seen - had *felt* - Jeff die. "What?"

Bill leaned forward. "He's going to be ok." He spoke the words slowly, with emphasis, as though trying to force them into Cole's head. "They're taking him to surgery, but they think they got to him in time and the Docs'll be able to patch him up. It'll be a tough recovery, but they seemed optimistic he'll be up and about good as new in a few months."

It was like a ten ton weight had been lifted. Cole breathed deeply, as though he had been underwater for five minutes. It felt like the first breath he had drawn in his life.

He was shaking, there in the car seat. Then he realized he was weeping, with relief, with joy.

"I don't know what we're going to do with you, Greg," Bill said. "Whether to give you a medal or bring you up on charges. Maybe both."

The words washed over Cole, but he paid them little heed.

Whatever else came from this night, his son was going to be ok. That was all that mattered.

Cole kept on crying. Slowly, though, his tears became laughter, and before long all that was all he could hear.

Bill watched him for a time, his expression that of a man who's not sure whether he is looking at madman or not. Then he opened the car door and got out.

Cole's laughter followed him.

Abe's Liquors

A Short Mystery

Michael Kingswood

Abe's Liquors

A young woman's quick trip to the liquor store turns unexpectedly exciting, and even more dangerous.

etty sniffed back tears and wiped the back of her right hand across the bottom of her nose. It had gone runny from crying so hard.

She squinted into the early evening darkness, her left hand flexing on the scarred and fading brown leather that wrapped the steering wheel of her Camry, and tried to concentrate on driving. But she couldn't get the fight out of her mind.

"Shut up, bitch!" and then the slap. Reeling backward as David stared hatred and disgust at her that the slap only confirmed. Fleeing from his apartment, though he did not follow. Stumbling down the stairs of his complex, tears making her vision blurry and sobs making her breathing difficult.

Then the frantic, near suicidal drive away.

She was twenty minutes further on now, and only just beginning to feel like she was getting herself back together. Slowly.

Ahead of her, a traffic light turned red, and she slowed to a stop.

Where was she?

When she had flown away from David's apartment complex, Betty had not paid any attention to where she was going, or even the traffic around her. Now she leaned forward, peering through her windshield, and could not recognize the area at all.

She was not in the suburbs any more, that was for sure. The buildings were closer together, cramped in. Mostly brick-faced, and there were neon business signs advertising a tavern, a his and hers barber shop, a thrift store. The cars parked on either side of the four-lane street were older than the part of town she was used to, and she could see small groups of people sitting on the porch steps of some of the buildings, just hanging out and talking.

Definitely not her neighborhood. And from the look of things, not all that great a neighborhood at all.

Still, she recognized the cross street at the intersection. Turn right here, and she should get back to highway in a few blocks. And then, in another twenty minutes or so, home.

Betty made the turn, and wiped at her nose again. She needed more tissues.

And she needed to get away from the depressing music on her Camry's radio. She hadn't even registered it consciously before now, but it was on a Top 40 station, and the singer was wailing out a ballad begging his girl to come back to him.

She punched the radio off before she burst into tears again, and drove on.

Ahead, the neighborhood continued pretty much as before, but she spied a sign coming up on the right. Abe's Liquor Store.

She didn't just need tissues. She needed a drink. Badly.

Betty was able to find a spot about fifty yards from the store, and took a couple minutes to parallel park her Camry between an old black Ford Explorer and a yellow Miata. She put the car into park and sat there for a moment, and looked herself in the mirror.

She was a mess. Her eyes were red and puffy, her mascara running. Her black hair, which she had carefully put up before going to meet David earlier, was mussed, strands pulled out from her barrettes.

She looked exactly what she was: a woman having a totally crappy evening.

Betty considered starting the car back up and just getting the hell out of there. But screw it. This wasn't her neighborhood; no one would know her to gossip about how messed up she was in the morning.

So she got out, smoothed the white skirt she was wearing, centered her green blouse more evenly on her shoulders, and strode up the street to the liquor store's door.

The sidewalk was cracked in a few places, the parking meters on the side of the street the old kind that only took coins and had those big twisty knobs to send the coins down into their containers; no debit cards or ApplePay for these. The liquor store itself had a long window at the front with posters of various beers and liquors posted up, and the front door was aluminum framed glass, with the standard broad paddle pull-to-open handle.

A bell rang over Betty's head when she stepped inside, and she immediately was struck by a musky incense from a lit burner behind the counter, which stood off to her left. It was wood-topped, and had the usual racks of last-minute purchase items on the customer side. The guy manning the register was in his thirties and Arabic-looking, with close-cropped black hair and a short beard. His off-white t-shirt had the store's name on the left breast.

When she walked in, the cashier looked her over quickly and nodded greeting when she met his eyes, then he went back to tending to his current customer, an elderly black woman in a white and blue polka-dotted dress and wide, gold-rimmed spectacles.

Turning away from the two of them, Betty saw three aisles filled with liquors and wines of all kinds, and at the back a full wall of refrigerated storage for beverages that needed to be ice-cold right now.

She walked to the second aisle, which looked to be more wine than anything else, and stepped past a tweed-jacketed white guy who looked to be in his fifties, with mostly grey hair and bright blue eyes. He shuffled to the side to let her pass with a smile and a polite, "Good evening."

It wasn't until she was three paces past him that his words registered, and she looked back to reply, but he was already queueing up behind the black woman.

Betty shook her head, upbraiding herself for being rude,

and shivered, only just now noticing how low the store had the air conditioning set.

Just get the wine, silly goose. You don't know these people, and they won't care what you did or didn't say ten minutes from now.

The whites were halfway down the aisle on the left, and Betty made a beeline for them. Reds were well and fine, but whites were so much more drinkable, and right then she needed something crisp and fruity, not something rich and deep.

She scanned the four levels of shelves quickly, stopping in surprise when a particular bottle sprang out at her. Yellow and white and red and orange and brown polygons all intertwined to make a regular pattern that seemed to draw the eye into its center. Alongside the pattern, the name: Coeur Sauvage, 2017 Loire Valley Sauvignon Blanc.

Betty remembered that particular bottle from a lunch out with four friends a month ago. Sally had revealed she was marrying Paul, and the five of them had splurged on more wine than they should have. But the Coeur stood out in her mind as being the best of the bottles they'd had.

She wet her lips in anticipation of the semi-sweet, slightly tangy flavor, and the warm buzz of relaxation the wine would bring.

That would do nicely.

Snatching the bottle up, Betty turned and headed toward the counter, where the tweed-jacketed guy was still waiting behind the old lady.

She was just finishing up when Betty got in line behind, hefting a paper bag that clinked from the sound of multiple bottles tapping together.

"Thank you," she said to the cashier and moved to the door.

The bell overtop the door rang before she got there, and a

tall broad-shouldered man with long brown hair half stepped in. Then, seeing the elderly woman coming his way, he stepped back out and held the door open for her.

The woman said, "Thank you, young man," and he smiled, nodded, and replied, "Of course, ma'am."

Once the old woman was past, he stepped back inside, and Betty got a better look at him. Late 20s probably. Wearing a brown leather jacket a couple shades darker than his hair, and jeans that looked like he'd had them for a while, doing actual work. Those worn parts were not fashion statements from a preppy clothing store.

He had dark, intelligent eyes and a bold nose. Square jaw. Nice looking fellow. His eyes met hers as he began moving toward the first aisle, and he smiled ever so slightly as they flicked quickly up and down her body.

Betty resolutely looked away from him, toward the cashier, who was just beginning to ring up tweed jacket's trio of wine bottles. She was in no mood for men, especially good looking men right -

The door swung open and the sound of the bell carried, along with the old woman's voice raised in a cry of alarm.

Betty looked left toward the door in time to see first one man, then a second, storm in. They were both dressed in long black pants and long-sleeved black t-shirts. They wore black gloves and black ski masks.

And they were both carrying silvery guns.

"Hands up!" shouted the first of the men, brandishing his gun—it was a revolver, Betty could see now—toward the cashier, who backed up behind his counter, hands raised.

He turned the gun toward tweed man and Betty, flicking it back and forth between then, and a shiver of fear went down her spine.

"Back up!"

She complied, as did tweed man.

The robber had a rolled-up cloth bag in his left hand, which he hurled toward the cashier. "Fill it!"

The cashier caught the bag and moved to comply, moving slowly and deliberately. Past the first robber, his partner was standing closer to the door, his gun on the handsome leather jacket guy. Leather jacket guy was standing ominously still, his hands raised, but his body was relaxed, like this was no big deal at all. His eyes were wary, but calm.

Betty tried to find some of that calm herself, but instead found only outrage. This was so, so…

She burst out. "You're robbing a liquor store? Seriously?? How cliche can you - ?"

The lead robber turned on her, and the barrel of his revolver pointed straight at her face. The silvery circle seemed to widen as she looked at it, the darkness inside the hole of the barrel opening up to suck her inside, and her bowels went to ice.

She was going to die. He was going to pull the trigger, and she was going to die. She could see the fingers holding his gun flex slightly, tensing for the killing movement.

Instead, he said, "Shut up, bitch." He shot her with his eyes, then turned his attention—and his gun—back to the cashier.

Shut up bitch.

The words rang in her ears, but she didn't hear the robber saying them. It was David again. Rage and disgust and hatred and disdain all mixed together in his tone, and eyes that smacked almost as hard as his hand had.

David, not the robber, and Betty's terror turned to a red-hot rage that flared up within her. How dare he?

She had the wine bottle in her hands. She moved without thinking, reversing her grip on it so she was holding it by the neck. Then, with a cry that carried all the rage, humiliation, and hurt she had been nursing the last half hour, she bound forward, raised the bottle high, and brought it down onto the robber's head.

It didn't shatter.

She thought it should have, but instead it struck with a dull, squishy thud and a jarring impact that ran up her arm to her shoulder before stabbing into her neck.

The robber dropped to the floor instantly, his body going limp. His gun made a metallic clink as it bounced once and landed on the floor tiles at Betty's feet.

Everything seemed to stop.

There was blood on the end of the bottle. She could see it in front of her eyes. She looked down and saw a trickle of blood flowing from the area of the man's head where she had struck him; the material of his ski mask was already soaked, and a little pool was beginning to form around his head on the floor.

His face was turned toward her, and she could see one of his eyes open wide, but glazed and unseeing. His jaw was slack.

Had she killed him? She hadn't meant to kill him. Hadn't meant to -

Sudden movement from off to the left drew Betty's attention away from the fallen man.

The second robber turned toward her, and leather jacket man sprang on him. The two men were wrestling, fighting over the gun.

Leather jacket man was taller, but the robber was well-muscled beneath his shirt, and Betty could tell leather jacket man had made a mistake. He'd over-extended, and was off balance even as the robber began pulling away from him.

He was going to fall, and the robber would win out. He would win out, and still have the gun. And when that happened, handsome leather jacket man would be dead. Maybe they all would be.

Betty cast about, and her eyes came to the first robber's revolver, lying at her feet.

She dropped the wine bottle and snatched up the gun. She'd never even held a gun, let alone fired one, and it was heavy in her hands. The knurled grip bit into her palm, and it seemed she shouldn't be able to lift it, so ominous did it feel.

She straightened and raised her eyes back to the conflict between the two men just in time to see leather jacket man land on his back on the floor. The robber moved quickly, placing his shoe onto the center of leather jacket man's chest.

He was bringing the gun around and down to point at his face -

"Stop!" Betty cried out, and she heard the quaver in her own voice. "Let him go."

Her hands were shaking, but she had the revolver pointed at the robber. She saw him stop, then look back at her. He straightened, and held his free hand out toward her, open and palm out in a gesture that was probably meant to be calming.

"Bitch, don't - "

The gun went off. She hadn't meant to fire. Hadn't realized she was squeezing the trigger under the gun bucked in her hands and the muzzle flash brightened in her eyes and the thunder of the bullet firing smashed her ears. They immediately began ringing.

Behind the robber was a shelf of vodka bottles. One immediately behind his head and just to the right shattered, and she realized she'd missed him.

Less than ten feet away, and she'd missed completely.

Part of her felt relief, because she didn't actually want to shoot him. The other part felt disgust, that she couldn't even manage to hit something that close.

The robber freaked. He jumped up half a foot and landed with his hands high in the air.

"Jesus," he said, and let his own pistol drop. "Jesus, don't - "

His eyes flicked toward the door, as though he was thinking about running.

Then he was on the floor, face smacking onto the tiles. Leather jacket man made some kind of scissor move with his legs that swept the robbers' legs out from under him, and then he was on top of the man, knee in the small of his back as he levered the man's arm up into a lock that had him squirming in pain. Both from the strain in his limb and from his nose, which was bleeding and looked to be broken.

Betty still had the revolver in her hands, but they were shaking more. Uncontrollably.

Fresh tears were streaming down her face, she realized, and her breathing was coming in quick heaves. Her heart was pounding in her ears, and sweat was making her blouse cling to her body.

But she couldn't let go of the gun.

A pair of hands closed around hers and she gave a little jerk. Then she realized it was tweed jacket man. He was speaking gently into her ear, and applying light pressure on her hands to move them downward.

"It's ok, miss. It's over. You can put the gun down now. It's over."

He said it in a low, drawling tone, almost the tone a parent would use when saying a lullaby to a child. At first she resisted lowering the gun. Then, all at once, her reserve—what reserve she had left—broke and she dropped it completely.

She sagged against tweed jacket man, sobbing, and he lowered her to the ground, leaning her back against the counter.

"Cops are on the way," she heard the cashier said from above and over her shoulder.

Tweed jacket man nodded, but remained where he was, squatting in front of her. "Do you need anything?"

She said the first thing that came to her mind. "Beer."

Tweed jacket man looked up past her toward the cashier. She could hear the shrug in his voice. "Give her a beer."

Tweed jacket man stood and hurried over to the refrigerated doors at the back of the store. She had seen earlier they held everything from cans of water that only claimed to be beer from their labels to good crafted ales. Right then, she'd take anything.

She looked away, back toward where leather jacket man had the robber in submission. He really was a nice looking fellow. Well built, too.

Leather jacket man looked up from the robber and met her eyes. He smiled again, more openly this time, and nodded at her.

Right then, she decided to get his phone number, and to hell with David.

The Billionaire's Daughter

A Davidson & Harper Mystery

Michael Kingswood

The Billionaire's Daughter

The strong-willed daughter of a wealthy man. The son of a notorious mob boss. And his grandmother's engagement ring.

Just another day on the job for private investigators Ronald Harper and Kathleen Davidson.

R onald checked his piece, tucked into a holster in the small of his back, then drew a deep breath and opened the door.

Warm light, muted music, and pleasant odors greeted him as he stepped inside. La Mer had a reputation as one of the best restaurants in town, and from the entryway alone, it looked to live up to it. Ronald felt underdressed in his khaki pants and leather jacket over a green collared shirt. Everyone else was in suits and evening gowns, or tuxedos.

The maitre d', a rotund man of around fifty who wore a formal tuxedo and presided over his domain from behind a mahogany lectern with the restaurant's logo engraved in the front, looked him up and down in disapproval. "Welcome to La Mer," he said in a lofty, I'm-better-than-you-and-we-both-know-it tone.

"Hello," Ronald said. "I'm meeting someone for dinner at seven thirty."

The maitre d's eyes flicked to the clock on the wall, and he frowned. "It is now seven forty-five, sir."

"I like to be fashionably late." Ronald winked at him.

"We have a strict dress code, sir. Sport coats and ties, no exception."

"Well, I'm sure that..."

"No exception!"

Shit. Now what? Ronald thought about trying to bribe his way in, but quickly dismissed that idea. This was the kind of place where they would call the cops on you for something like that.

"We do have coats and ties you may rent for the evening, if you wish," said the maitre d'.

"You do?"

The other man shrugged. "It is not an extensive collection, but you may find something that will fit." He gestured off to the left, where a homely young lady in a white collared shirt and black pants manned the restaurant's coat closet. Ronald could see a number of overcoats on the racks there, but few blazers. Oh well, never know til you try.

"Thanks," he said and turned away.

"Certainly, sir," came the pompous reply from astern.

Ronald was in luck. They had one coat in his size, 46 Regular. And wonder of wonders, it was not completely hideous. The tie was another matter entirely; it clashed with both his shirt and the coat. Beggars can't be choosers though, so he accepted both and soon enough he was dressed "appropriately", though quite a bit lighter in the wallet. The rental fee was outrageous.

He walked past the maitre d' and into the restaurant proper, trying hard to keep his normal swagger.

La Mer's layout was fairly typical: a bar manned by a pair of white-shirted bartenders at the front, with the dining area further back. It was the design of the place that set it apart. The bar was topped in marble and a quick glance showed only top-shelf liquors in their selection. The dining area reeked of opulence beneath the sumptuous odors of the varied dishes laid out for the customers' consumption. The walls were carved into faux-columns at regular intervals, with numerous paintings that Ronald was sure cost more than his monthly paycheck hanging between them. The furnishing was simple, but carried those little touches of detail that screamed quality if you knew what you were looking at.

It was definitely not his kind of place.

Many eyes followed him as he weaved through the tables. He tried to tell himself it was on account of his dashing good looks and not because he looked ridiculous in his new coat and tie. Himself was hearing none of it, though.

Fortunately, he did not have far to go. He spied Kathleen at a table near the windows, about a third of the way back. She, of course, was dressed to kill in a blue evening gown that matched her eyes, along with a diamond necklace and earrings. She watched him coming with a highly amused expression on her face.

"Good evening," he said as he came to a stop next to her table. "Mind if I join you?"

"I'm not sure I'm worthy to be in the presence of so striking a man."

Ronald rolled his eyes. He sat down across the table from her but stopped for a moment in surprise. "Damn, this is the most comfortable restaurant chair I've ever sat in," he said.

Kathleen quirked an eyebrow upward and shook her head at him. "This *is* La Mer."

"Yeah." Ronald scowled at a prissy little fellow in a tuxedo at the next table over who was staring at him in revulsion. The little guy flinched and looked away quickly. "You could have warned me about the dress code."

Kathleen sniffed. "I assumed you would have the sense to look into it yourself," she replied. "But apparently not."

"Whatever."

The waiter, also dressed in a white collared shirt and black pants - Ronald was beginning to detect a trend - appeared next to the table then with an empty wine glass, which he filled from the bottle already on the table. Opus One, very nice. Whoever the client was, he must have deep pockets.

"Would you like to hear the specials, sir?"

Kathleen made a dismissive little wave with her hand. "No, please," she said before Ronald could speak. The waiter bowed slightly from the waist and departed.

"I actually wanted to hear them."

She sniffed again. "The hell you did. You're going to order a steak, medium, with garlic mashed potatoes and broccoli. Just like always."

Ronald nodded, conceding the point, then lifted his wine glass. "To us," he said.

She smirked, but lifted her glass in turn. The glasses rang like a pair of little bells as they met for the toast. They spare no expense at La Mer, it seemed. No big surprise. He took a long drink from his glass, savoring the exquisite flavor for a moment before swallowing.

"So," he said, turning his head to survey the crowd. "Who's the mark?"

"See the older gentleman..."

"Which one? It's like a geriatric convention in here."

Kathleen was silent for a long moment. Ronald could feel the irritation, and the disapproval, in her stare though he did not look back at her. Finally, she started over.

"Table for six, third from the back along the far wall."

Ronald found it easily. Two men in tuxedos, one in his sixties and the other maybe twenty-five at most, sat in the company of four young ladies in evening gowns. Three of the ladies were a bit plump for his taste, but the last was a hot little brunette number in a green dress, who could have been taken straight from the pages of Playboy. Ronald did a doubletake to make sure he was seeing clearly.

"Who the hell are *they*?"

"They," Katheleen said, "are Marcus Romero and his children."

Wow. That guy had some great genetics, apparently. Wait a minute.

"Marcus Romero the oil tycoon?"

Kathleen nodded.

Ronald whistled softly. Romero was high up on the Forbes 500. If he was the target...

"He's a pretty heavy hitter, Kat. Are you sure about this?"

"It's a job like any other. You're not scared, are you?"

Damn right he was scared. Some people you did *not* mess with. Not without some serious backing. Of course, he was not about to admit that to Kathleen. At least, not yet.

"What's the job?"

She held up one finger and pursed her lips slightly. A few seconds later, the waiter returned and inquired about their order. Ronald ordered his usual, evoking an amused grin from Kathleen, who ordered seared Ahi with mashed potatoes and a side salad. The waiter bowed again and left.

"Apparently," Kathleen said after taking another sip of wine, "Romero's youngest daughter, Isabel, was recently engaged to be married. She called it off but refused to give back the engagement ring."

Ronald looked at her incredulously. "You're kidding."

Kathleen shook her head.

"So our job is to recover a stupid engagement ring from a billionaire's daughter? Christ just buy another one." Seriously, at the rates he and Kathleen charged, that would be far cheaper.

"It's not just any engagement ring. It's a family heirloom of some substantial value."

"Ok, so hire a lawyer. Why us?"

"The former fiancee is...connected." She put special emphasis on the word connected. What was...Aw shit.

Ronald groaned. "Really? She was engaged to a mobster?"

"That is the reason she broke it off. But apparently this particular mobster used his grandmother's engagement ring for the proposal, and didn't tell his father about it beforehand. So..."

"If he makes a big legal stink about it, daddy finds out and maybe he sends some boys over to break her kneecaps to get it back."

Kathleen nods. "He still loves her he says, and doesn't want to see anything bad happen to her. But he *needs* the ring back." She spread her hands and smiled cheerfully. "And so, here we are."

"They must not have been engaged very long, if Daddy didn't meet her and see the ring."

Kathleen shook her head. "About six months."

That didn't make any sense. "Then how..."

"Daddy is Johnny Palmieri."

"Ah." Palmieri was doing five years for racketeering. His son Mario was supposedly running things while Johnny was in the can, but everyone knew Johnny still got regular reports and called a lot of the shots. Ronald looked back at Romero's table and took another drink of wine. "Which one is Isabel?"

"In green."

Ronald grinned. "Lord, I was hoping you were going to say that."

Kathleen rolled her eyes, but Ronald could tell it was from amusement more than disapproval.

There was not much else to say about it, so Ronald took another drink and leaned back in his chair. Might as well enjoy dinner. Lord knew when he would ever have the chance to eat at La Mer again.

Dinner was exquisite, exceeding his every expectation. The meat was perfectly prepared and seasoned, and seemed to melt in his mouth, it was so tender. It was hard to keep an eye on the Romero table with such a feast in front of him. But he was a professional, so he managed.

They finished eating several minutes before Kathleen and he did, but made no move to get up. Perhaps they had ordered desert, or were meeting friends? Regardless, their finishing was a sign for him and Kathleen to go. The trick was to finish and go without appearing to rush, which would have drawn attention.

Kathleen handled the check, then they were off. Five minutes later, they sat in Ronald's car in the parking lot, watching the entrance through a couple of small binoculars Ronald kept under his car seat.

"She has her own place, right?"

"She's twenty-four years old. I certainly hope she does," Kathleen replied.

"You never know with these rich girls... Ok, there she is."

Isabel's dress was easy to spot. She came out after the rest of her family and hung back from them while they waited for the valets to retrieve their vehicles.

"How long ago did she break it off with mob-boy?"

"About a month ago."

"Hmm. Looks like the rest of the family may be giving her the cold shoulder over it."

Beside him, Kathleen snickered.

One by one, the Romeros got in their cars and drove away, until only Marcus himself and Isabel remained. Through the binoculars, they appeared to be talking heatedly about something. Isabel was wagging a finger in his face; she was pissed! Then a blue Boxter pulled up and a valet got out. Isabel snatched the key out of the valet's hand and got in, then sped off out of the parking lot and down the street. Marcus slumped, clearly upset or resigned about whatever had just transpired, and turned away.

"Poor guy," Ronald mused.

"Yeah, I'm crying a river for him. Get after her!"

Ronald grinned at Kathleen. Leave it to her to suppress empathy beneath professionalism. But she was right. He started up the engine and pulled out onto the street.

The Boxter was already a block ahead of them, and moving at a high rate of speed. There was no way Ronald could overtake Isabel in his Outback. But then, he did not have to. As long as he kept her in sight, it was all good.

But that was easier said than done. Isabel veered around corners at breakneck speed and zoomed in and out of traffic like a madwoman. She must really have been pissed off. Or at least, Ronald hoped that was why she was driving like that. Otherwise, she was a highway fatality waiting to happen.

He lost sight of her for a panicked minute as she zoomed around two turns in quick succession. Only Kathleen looking down a side-street and spotting her saved the night. Eventually, she slowed down as she got into the more opulent area of town. Single family houses gave way to mansions, and she assumed a more stately pace. Don't want to piss off the neighbors, after all.

Finally, she pulled into a circular driveway in front of a large but not over-the-top house backing up to a small lake, probably man-made. Ronald pulled to a stop a few houses...mansions...away, made a note of the address, and broke out the binoculars again.

Isabel stormed into the house, leaving the front door wide open. She remained out of sight for almost fifteen minutes. When she came back out, Ronald almost did not recognize her. She wore cut-off blue jeans and a white t-shirt with a logo or design of some sort on the front. Her hair was pulled back in a ponytail and she had discarded most of her jewelry.

"She could almost pass for a real person," Kathleen observed from the seat beside Ronald.

He laughed.

Isabel got back into the Boxter and pulled out of the driveway, then turned left and drove back toward downtown.

Thirty minutes later, Ronald led Kathleen into a dimly-lit nightclub. Bearing the super-original name The Techno, the place was much like every other nightclub Ronald had ever been in, if perhaps a bit on the seedy side. The same annoying "dance" music thumped over the speakers as in every other place, loud enough to make conversation difficult in anything less than a shout. The bar was battered, with scratches in the counter and stickers of various sorts posted all over. It held a standard low-brow booze selection and sat in the predictable location over on the right. The dance floor was in back beneath multi-colored spotlights, with the DJ station on a raised platform off to the left above the floor. The place smelled of booze and sweat, and the floor was sticky in spots from spilled drinks, and possibly other fluids Ronald did not want to think about.

Overall, not a very inspiring location, and not the sort of place Ronald would have expected a spoiled little rich girl to frequent. Kathleen was over-dressed for it. But not by much. Many of the women there were dressed up in club attire. Still, Ronald noticed a few people eyeing her askance. Best not to keep her here for long. He got the impression this was not always the safest place.

Isabel seemed to like it, though. Ronald spotted her after a minute's looking, shaking it up on the dance floor with abandon. Men and women danced around her, but she did not appear to be with any of them. Ronald continued to watch her as he and Kathleen meandered over to the bar, and she gave no less than three guys the brush-off.

"Ok, now what?"

Ronald looked at Kathleen and grinned. "I'll keep her busy here. You go search her place." He held out the keys to his car.

Kathleen looked incredulously at him. "You're going to keep her busy."

"Yup."

She snorted. "Now this I have to see."

Ronald shook his head. "No, now you need to get out of here." He leaned closer. "You're a bit over-dressed."

Kathleen scowled, but she nodded. She was a professional, after all. "Alright." She snatched the keys from Ronald's hand. "Text me when she's on her way home. I don't want to be there when she gets back."

Ronald nodded and gave her a little salute, then he turned and headed out to the dance floor.

Some men have trouble meeting women in clubs. Ronald was not one of them. He had no idea why. Maybe it was the fact that he actually knew how to dance; several years of ballroom training back in Junior High and High School still paid dividends. Maybe it was because he acted like a gentlemen. Or maybe it was just his jacket. Either way, after a few minutes dancing around, he maneuvered closer to Isabel, and sure enough, she flashed him a smile.

Sometimes it was just too easy.

They danced together for five songs before she stepped off the dance floor, gesturing toward the bar. Ronald followed. She ordered a scotch and soda. Ronald mulled it over and went with a seven and seven, earning a look of amusement from her.

"What?" he asked, "You don't like Seven-Up?"

Isabel shrugged. "From the way you dance, I figured you for something a bit stronger."

Ronald wasn't sure how to take that, to be honest. It was not often he found himself without a pithy comeback, but just then he had nothing.

"Well, I like a seven and seven sometimes."

Isabel laughed and ran her hand down his arm. "Don't be grumpy. I didn't mean anything."

"It would be easier to take if I knew your name. I'm Ron."

"Isabel."

They shook hands, and the bartender brought back their drinks. Ron reached for his wallet, but Isabel placed her hand over his, preventing him from taking it out of his pocket.

"I've got this one," she said. "Payback for the dances."

"Far be it from me to pass up a drink from a lovely lady."

Isabel laughed again. It was a good sign when he made a woman laugh. Well, usually. He was not joking though. She was great-looking in the restaurant, and from afar. Up close, she was stunning. And that was dressed-down. He could understand mob-boy's affection, though he was surprised a guy like that would so readily let a girl like her go.

They sipped their drinks and exchanged small talk for a while. Or as best they could with all the music blaring in their ears anyway. She worked as a commodities trader in the local exchange. Liked running and was training for a triathlon. Had a dog once, but after he died could never bring herself to get another one. Enjoyed travel; Prague was her favorite foreign city. Spoke Spanish and German. She never mentioned her billionaire father, though; smart of her.

Ronald answered questions about himself as they came, but for the most part let her do the talking. He had found that people enjoyed talking about themselves, and would happily do so with just a bit of prodding. It made his line of work a whole lot easier, that was for sure. All at once, though, she stopped talking and looked over his shoulder at something. Then her eyes widened slightly and she slouched down against the bar, pushing closer to him. She was using him as concealment from someone in the rear of the club, Ronald realized quickly.

"What's wrong?"

Isabel replied in a strained voice, "Those three guys are friends of my ex. Shit, they never come here!"

Ronald looked over his shoulder and instantly saw who she was talking about. Three guys, not particularly big but obviously muscular, dressed sharply but in the sort of way that screams ,"Gumbah". They stood near the door, surveying the scene like hunters seeking out prey.

"Have they been giving you problems?" Ronald looked back at her. He would lose track of what they were doing by looking away, but it would be worse to make eye contact; it would just draw attention to himself, and her. Moving casually, he repositioned himself slightly, to afford her better cover as well.

Isabel nodded, keeping her head down.

"All right. Let's get out of here." Ronald took hold of Isabel's arm gently. "Follow me and do exactly what I say, ok?"

She looked up at him. There was fear in her eyes, but also confusion laced with curiosity. Who was this guy who was suddenly trying to play the hero? Ronald could practically hear the thought streaming through her head.

"I have a bit of experience with these sorts of situations. Will you trust me?"

She hesitated, then nodded.

"Ok. Get your car keys out."

Ronald glanced back at the Gumbahs. They had moved away from the exit and were making their way toward the dance floor, spread out so they could cover more area. The closest one would be in a position to see Isabel in a few seconds.

"When I say, run to the exit as fast as you can. I'll be right behind you."

The Gumbah was close. It was now or never.

"Get ready," Ronald said, then he turned and, moving in a lurch as though he was drunk, stumbled headlong into the Gumbah.

"Get off me, motherfucker!" The Gumbah shoved him. Hard.

Ronald stumbled backward a step, then threw up his hands and said, "Hey man, I'm sorry man," making sure to slur his words. The Gumbah looked at him in disgust. Then the thug's eyes widened as he recognized Isabel behind Ronald. He stepped forward, toward her.

"Go!" As he shouted, Ronald kicked as hard as he could. His foot connected with the side of the Gumbah's knee. He could not hear the sound of bone or ligaments snapping over the roar of the speakers, but from the way the thug dropped instantly, grabbing at his knee and rolling with an agonized expression on his face, Ronald knew he had caused some major damage.

He did not wait to see if the other two had noticed or not. He turned and raced toward the entrance. Isabel was already out the door; she could be quick when she needed to, it seemed.

Ronald brushed past the bouncer at the door and scurried up the stairs to street level, shoving past individuals and one small group who were on their way down and earning chagrined curses from one and all. Better than getting shot in the back. Bursting through the door, he stumbled to a stop outside and looked around.

The parking lot stood, about two thirds full, across the street from the club's building. Clubbers, dressed for the party and laughing up a storm, congregated around cars, either just arriving or getting ready to leave. The street stretched left and right for several blocks before turning, with darkened buildings at intervals on either side.

Isabel was nowhere to be seen. Shit.

Frantically looking left and right, he saw movement in the alley entrance next the building. She could not be that stupid, could she? He darted toward the alley and just got around the corner enough to make out a white shirt, jeans, and a female's shape when something slammed into his cheek from the side. Hard.

He went down in a heap, his head ringing and his cheek already beginning to swell painfully. Then a boot struck him in the gut, sending him rolling over into a couple of trash cans, upending one of them and sending refuse spilling out all around him. He lay there, stunned, tasting his own blood from where he bit his lip in the impact and trying not to absorb the stink of the spilled trash.

Isabel let out a panicked shout and ran. He could hear the sound of her light footfalls receding into the alley. Larger, heavier footsteps followed. At least they didn't stay to beat on him.

Sudden fury, at himself and at the situation, flared within Ronald, and he forced himself to roll back over onto his belly and place his hands beneath himself. He had to stop there for a few seconds while the world stopped spinning. Then he took a deep breath and pushed himself up onto his hands and knees. It felt like he was lifting the world, but it worked.

He raised his head. The alley contained no streetlights, but he could make out some details from the lights in the parking lots across the street. Two bulky forms stood near the wall about halfway down the alley. One of them was pushing a smaller body, Isabel he was certain, up against the wall by her throat. Ronald heard a deep voice saying something, but the thug was talking low enough that he could not make out the words.

Ronald took another deep breath. Time for that hero bit. Why did it always have to be the hero bit?

He forced himself up to his feet, using the trash can for support along the way, and stood swaying for as long as he dared. Which was not long, with Isabel alone with those two. He checked his holster - yep still there - and drew his Glock, then moved down the alley toward Isabel and the Gumbahs as quickly as he could.

"...wants it back."

"Fuck you, Marty. It's mine." Ronald had to give it to her, Isabel was tough. Maybe not the smartest ever, but tough.

Marty, the Gumbah doing the talking, drew back as though to hit her.

"That's about enough of that, Marty," Ronald said, drawing a bead on him over the sights of his Glock.

The Gumbahs both turned their heads in surprised anger that quickly gave way to nervous wariness when they saw Ronald's gun. For a second, everyone stood perfectly still, the thugs clearly considering whether he was willing to shoot and Isabel looking at him with a mixture of surprise, gratitude, and hope.

"Alright Marty, have your pal let her go, then both of you put your hands up and back away, nice and slow."

Ronald learned the tone of voice that makes people obey without question in the Marines Corps. It worked just as well on these Gumbahs as it had on wet-behind-the-ears privates from flyover country. They released Isabel and backed up as commanded, but scowled darkly at him.

"You're digging your own grave, you know that, mother-fucker?" Marty said.

Ronald shrugged. "Maybe." Glancing aside at Isabel, he said, "Still got your keys?"

She nodded, her eyes still wide with fright. She was trembling visibly.

"Go get your car and pull it to the front of the alley."

She nodded again. Pausing only to say, "Thank you," in a voice that trembled as much as her arms and legs did, she hurried away.

Once she was out of earshot, it was time to talk business. "Johnny Palmieri sent you guys to get the ring back, huh?"

Marty blinked, surprise flashing across his features, then he nodded.

"Thought so. Look, you tell him his son will have the ring back to him by the end of the week, ok? Until then, leave the girl alone."

Marty just scowled. That was probably the best Ronald was going to get, so he began slowly backing away from them, toward the mouth of the alley. He was almost there when, with a screeching of tires, the Boxter came to a halt and its passenger door popped open. He breathed a sigh of relief; he had not been entirely sure she was going to come back for him.

"Tell your buddy sorry about his knee," he called out to the

Gumbahs, then he leapt into the car and slammed the door shut. "Drive. Fast."

In retrospect, the last part of the order was neither required nor desired. Isabel floored it, and the Boxter surged ahead with more acceleration than he had ever experienced in a car before. Goddamn, this ride was sweet. Ronald twisted around in his seat and saw the thugs rush out of the alley behind them, but they did not pursue, at least not immediately.

"Looks like we're in the clear," he reported.

Isabel nodded, her eyes flickering from the rearview mirror to him and then back to the street ahead. "Are you a cop?"

Ronald shook his head and slid his hips forward on the seat so he could re-holster his Glock. "I'm a Private Investigator."

She blinked, then shook her head and laughed, sounding almost like the girl he had talked to at the bar again. "You're kidding. Like in the movies?"

"Something like that. Look," Ronald fixed her with the most serious look he knew how to give. "You really need to give Mario Palmieri his grandmother's ring back."

Isabel's eyes widened and she slammed on the brakes. The car fishtailed briefly as it slowed then came to a halt, and Ronald had to press his palms against the dashboard to avoid being thrown into the windshield.

"Are you fucking kidding me? You too? You need to get the fuck out of this car, right now!"

"Isabel, listen to me..."

"GET OUT!"

Ronald did not reach for the door handle. "Mario gave that ring to you without..."

She made as if to slap him, but Ronald caught her hand in mid-swing and held it still in a firm grip at the wrist.

"He gave it to you without his father's permission. He hired me and my partner to get it back from you because he didn't want his father finding out and doing something bad to you." She tried to pull back, but he tightened his grip on her wrist. She winced, but made no sound. "It looks like he found out anyway; that's why Marty and his buddies were after you tonight. The only way out of this is to give it back."

It's also the required thing to do when you dump a guy after you've agreed to marry him, Ronald did not say.

Isabel was silent for a full minute, scowling at him the whole time. Then, finally, she blew his mind.

"So that whole bit on the dance floor and at the bar was bullshit?" Were their tears in her eyes? "Dammit, I *liked* you."

Ronald could not remember when he had been so surprised. He released Isabel's wrist and dropped his hand into his lap, unsure what to say for a moment. Ah fuck it, just be straight up. "Not completely. Yes, I was there for the job. But I like you also. And I *sure* don't want to see anything bad happen to you."

Isabel stared at him, saying nothing. Ronald began to wonder if she was going to get out of the car herself or something silly like that. But then she sighed and nodded.

"It's an ugly ring, anyway."

She put the car into gear and sped off down the road again.

Ronald laughed in spite of himself. "Then why the hell did you not give it back to begin with?"

"Principle."

"Come again?"

Isabel glanced at him, looking a trifle annoyed. "Principle. He lied to me the whole time we were together. He makes his living by hurting other people." She took a deep breath, then said in a somewhat petulant tone, "I just thought he should suffer a little bit himself."

Ronald was forced to admit, there was a certain logic and poetic justice about that train of thought. Pity they lived in the real world, where trying that sort of thing is likely to get a person hurt or killed. But still a halfway decent thought.

"Where do you keep it?"

"In a safe at work where we keep our client information. Very secure."

"Alright. Let's go."

Isabel shook her head. "It's a double-combination safe, and I only have one of them." Her lips turned up into a sly grin and she raised an eyebrow at him. "Very secure."

She was not kidding. Ronald had seen a couple safes like that in the Corps, but they were only used for highly classified stuff like crypto. Her firm took protection of their customer information seriously. He made a mental note to look into the requirements to open an account there. Later.

"Ok. Then first thing in the morning, get it and bring it by my office." He reached into the inner pocket of his leather jacket and pulled out a business card, which he laid on the center console.

Isabel pursed her lips. "How do I know you'll get it to Mario? Maybe I should just bring it to him myself."

That would make it hard for me to get paid, Ronald didn't say. "Remember, his father's goon's are looking for you. That could get pretty ugly. And besides," he looked quizzically at her, "do you *really* want to see Mario again? He's just going to beg you to come back to him, you know."

Isabel considered that and nodded. "You've got a point. Alright, your office at ten o'clock?"

"Sure."

"It's a date." She flashed him a quick smile that made a little shiver of excitement run down Ronald's spine. She was a little minx, wasn't she? "So where should I drop you off?"

Ronald was half-tempted to suggest her place, just to see what could happen. But his wiser head prevailed and he gestured toward the card. "My office will be fine."

Isabel nodded silently. Was that disappointment that he saw in her eyes for a second? Surely not.

He settled back into the sculpted car seat, and they drove in silence the rest of the way to his building. He and Kathleen rented a small office on the second floor of a little commercial building downtown. A drug store and a falafel joint dominated the sign space out front, so it was very easy to miss the little sign that read "Davidson and Harper, Private Investigators" next to a narrow glass door at the end of the building.

Isabel pulled to a stop and looked his building over for a moment. "Well, here we are."

"Yep." Ronald opened the car door. "See you at ten."

"I'll be there," she smiled. Then she leaned over and gave him a light kiss on the cheek. The brush of her lips sent another rush of excitement through him. "Thanks again for helping me with those guys," she said as she pulled back from the kiss, her breath hot against his cheek.

Ronald swallowed hard and put on his best nonchalant smile. Or at least he hoped it was nonchalant. "My pleasure," he said. Their eyes met, and he felt drawn into hers. He had not noticed the flecks of yellow buried in the green of her irises before. She really did have nice...

He broke that chain of thought and looked away, clearing his throat. "Until tomorrow then," he said, somewhat lamely. Then he got out of the car and closed the door. He thought he saw her smile in amusement for a moment before she pulled away.

It was only when he was unable to open that little glass door leading up to his office that he remembered he did not have his keys. And that he had not texted Kathleen yet.

She was going to be pissed.

Hunting
For Game
A Short Crime Story
Michael
Kingswood

Hunting For Game

From a secluded hunting blind that no one else knows about, a man goes hunting for more than just game.

George opened up the trunk of his blue Ford Focus and hefted a brown canvas duffle bag out. He shifted his torso, slinging the duffle over his left shoulder, and grunted softly at the weight of the bag's contents. He'd thrown that shoulder out once about five years earlier while weight lifting, and sometimes he had flare-ups from it. He hadn't had one in a while…until just this moment.

Wasn't that just great.

George gritted his teeth and slammed the trunk shut, then hit the key fob to lock the car up and turned away.

He was parked off of a two-lane country road that had departed from the main highway three miles back the way he'd come. The road had twisted and turned through rolling hills covered with lush green forest until he'd reached this spot, and he'd pulled off behind a billboard sign for a roadhouse bar and grill ten miles farther on.

Stepping out from behind the billboard, he glanced left and right; no one was around. That was good. He'd be out in his stand for several hours, probably. It was his secret place, and he didn't want anyone to find where it was, or know that he was even here.

That could be bad, and mess up his afternoon. And more.

He also had three grand in cash stashed in the cardboard box that had ridden in the trunk with the duffle. Better not to risk losing that if someone broke into the car, or stole it.

Hence, the concealed parking job.

He'd been out of the car's air conditioning for less than a minute, but already sweat was beginning to trickle down his back from the mid-summer heat and the humidity that made the air feel thick and smell of moisture. Overhead, puffy white clouds moved briskly across the sky from west to east, in the direction he had to walk, and he watched one go out of sight behind the tress atop the hill he needed to climb.

Then he adjusted the duffle and hurried across to the other side of the road and beneath the forest canopy beyond.

Immediately it became more dim, but it didn't cool at all. If possible it seemed to warm up, actually.

George slowed as soon as he was out of sight of the road, and began ascending the hill, being careful to avoid trip hazards as he scanned the tree trunks for the signs he had left earlier. Where was - ?

There. Carved into a trunk thirty feet to the left. A heart with the letters G + H inside.

He strode over and laid his hand atop the rough bark, trailing his fingers around the carving he had made a week ago. They traced the heart, then brushed past his initial to the H, and there they stopped.

As it always did when he thought about Heather, his heart wrenched in his chest and he found himself gasping, suddenly breathless.

The image came to him of her, thirteen years old with her dark brown hair tied into two pigtails, dressed in a yellow sun dress and beaming an ear to ear smile on the day he'd taken her to see that movie she'd been asking him about for weeks. Why couldn't he remember its name now? If had been so important to her, and it had only been two years ago. Why - ?

Then he flashed to the last time he'd seen her face, how different it had looked from that happy day, and his gasping breathing became a sob that he had to work to contain.

He leaned forward and pressed forehead against the tree trunk, and forced his emotions down. He drew in a long, deep breath. Held it, and counted to ten.

Then he pushed himself back upright and, wiping his nose with the back of his right hand, he turned back upslope and resumed his trek.

The hill wasn't particularly steep, but it was a long ascent and by the time he reached the crest George was breathing heavily and sweating up a storm. But it wasn't far now, so he pressed on down the back side.

He reached his hide five minutes later.

It had taken him weeks to find this one perfect place, and then more time to get it built. Fifteen feet up the trunk of a towering sycamore, balanced in the gap between the trunk and a branching limb, the hide was a wooden platform large enough for George to lie prone comfortably.

He'd driven planks into the trunk to act as ladder rungs, and he took a moment to re-situate the duffle over both his shoulders, like a pack. Then he boosted himself up into the tree.

Once he was up, George dropped the duffle with a sigh of relief and rolled his shoulders. He was getting too old for this.

But he had to do it, for Heather's sake if nothing else.

She'd begun to come with him on his hunting trips, and had started to appreciate them, before -

Again he flashed to the last time he'd seen her, on the flat stainless steel, covered by a blue sheet that the orderly had pulled back so he could see her face. Bruised, cut, battered. Staring blankly into the bright lights of the ceiling, but not seeing them.

Not seeing anything.

George flopped down onto the wood that he had shaped and sanded, and laid into place here. His rump hit the platform, and he leaning forward, elbows on his knees as he pressed his hands to his eyes, willing himself not to see.

But still the image of his little girl would not go away.

He tried to think of another time, a happier time. But it wouldn't come. In his minds eye, his daughter's dead, lifeless eyes turned toward him, and he heard her voice in his head.

"Why didn't you protect me, daddy?"

George jerked upright, and heard himself scream for a second before he forced himself back to silence.

Don't scare away the game. Though that was extremely unlikely, here. In this place. For this game.

George drew a deep breath, then turned and unzipped the duffle bag. Along with his other gear, he had a gallon jug of water in the bag. He pulled it out and drank deeply.

The water had warmed since he took it out of his refrigerator two hours earlier, but even still it was cool compared with the heat of the day. The coolness spread down his throat and into his belly, and he let out a long sigh as he set the jug down.

Through a gap in the trees ahead of him, a glint of light drew his attention, and he leaned forward again, squinting. The lake, below and a few hundred yards away from his position, was rippling with waves, and the sunlight glinted at intervals off it.

Smiling thinly, George nodded to himself, then got to work on the rest of his gear.

The rifle was bolt action, chambered in .308 Remington, with a telescopic sight. He'd taken lots of game with it over the years. Lord willing, today would yield even greater results.

He pulled a box of ammo and a bipod mount out of the bag, then set to screwing the mount onto the lug at the bottom of the rifle barrel.

As he worked, his mind wandered back again. But not to the morgue, and Heather.

Three months, later, and sitting down with the detectives and prosecutor assigned the case. They'd caught the guy, had him dead to rights. The prosecutor would seek the death penalty, but probably he'd end up with life without parole. So at least he wouldn't be able to kidnap, rape, and murder any other little girls.

The earlier smile faded into a scowl as George remembered going into the courthouse for the pre-trial hearings. Watching as the defense attorney submitted a motion to dismiss.

And then stunned disbelief when the judge granted it, with prejudice.

George's scowl became a grimace as he set the rifle down, the bipod holding the barrel up off the floor now, and opened up the ammo box. He loaded four rounds into the ammo receiver, then jammed the bolt home, chambering a round. He checked the safety on, then arranged himself into a prone position, rifle butt snug into his right shoulder.

He recalled spending a week in jail. Contempt of court from the protests he'd shouted when the judge dismissed the case.

Seeing the prosecutor after he got out, and learning the perp was the nephew of a State Senator, or something.

He flipped off the dust covers over his sights and pressed his cheek against the stock.

Distant tree trunks and underbrush leaped into view in his eye, slightly blurry. He adjusted the focus ever so slightly, then panned the rifle left and right on the bipod, testing its function.

Smooth and easy.

He'd pressed the prosecutors to try again, maybe in a different venue, a different judge. But dismissing with prejudice meant the case could never be pressed again, period.

He walked out of the prosecutor's office, feeling his entire world crumble apart.

First Jane, four years earlier. Now Heather. Both had been murdered: his wife by cancer, and his girl -

George blinked away tears and focused on the sights as he shifted his aim point toward the break in the trees.

There could be no justice for Jane. But there should have been for Heather. And that had been stolen; from her and from him.

Through the sight, he saw the lake again. The ripples running across its surface were stronger, originating from just to the left of his field of view. Shifting his aim slightly, he saw the boat whose wake had been creating the ripples. It had a white hull and blue bimini above its conning station. It was sleek and lacked any superstructure: a speed boat.

And sure enough, it was pulling a bikini-clad woman behind it, on waterskis.

George wanted to smile at the sight, but he couldn't bring himself to. He shifted further to the left, and the lake's shore sprang into view. Large houses—mansions, practically—lined the water's edge. Some were sided in brick, some in more conventional planks, but all had the look of places that had been built in the last ten years or so. Each had a dock, and was separated from its neighbor by a fence that ran to the waterline.

A few had swimming pools in their yards above the lake, and wasn't that silly. All had meticulously-pruned landscaping, and lawn furniture for entertaining.

The house halfway down the lake's edge toward him had another boat just tying up to the dock. A dark-haired man in a white shirt and tan shorts was just standing from cleating off the boat's lines. The sun reflected off the lenses of his sunglasses quickly as he turned back to the boat and reached out to help its other two passengers out onto the dock.

They were a woman, somewhat plump but tall, almost as tall as the man, in a pink and white sun dress, and a girl; though young woman would be a better term from the growing hips that were plainly visible from the one-piece blue swimsuit she was wearing. She had brown hair, like her mother, and stopped to slip on Daisy Dukes before stepping off the boat.

The trio walked up the dock to a paved patio area a few yards up from the lake's edge, to where a glass-topped patio table surrounded by four white slatted chairs waited for them.

The man and the young lady sat down, and the woman hurried up to the house. She returned a few moments later, carrying a tray with a pitcher filled with a yellowish fluid—

lemonade?—and three glasses. Her face was in view now that she was returning, and despite her sunglasses George recognized her with ease.

Judge Madelin Rosenburg.

The woman who had dismissed the case and thrown him in jail. The woman who had denied Heather her justice.

George tracked her as she walked back to the table, keeping his sighting reticle on her the whole way, and licked his lips.

He had been watching her, and her family, for months. Learning her patterns. Searching for an opening. It hadn't been particularly hard to learn about this lake house, when they tended to come here, and for how long. The Judge didn't have any social media accounts, but her sister did.

And so did her daughter.

Between the multitude of postings and check-ins those two had sent out to anyone with the desire and wherewithal to look, he knew where to go.

That just left finding the right place from which to hunt his game. That had really been the long pole. A place that was within the effective range of his rifle, and within his ability to get a hit, and was secluded enough that he could be assured of being able to make an escape.

Truth be told he really didn't care all that much about getting away. If he got caught, so be it. But it would be better to make a clean getaway.

He'd finally found the sycamore, and the gap in the trees that offered precisely the right angle. Then it was just a matter of waiting for Labor Day on the lake.

He kept tabs on the good Judge in the interim, and went to the range frequently to get his marksmanship up to the best it could be.

Now it was time. The game was in the open, and he had his shot.

Justice for Heather. Finally.

The Judge poured cups for her husband and daughter, then sat down in a chair facing George's position, to her husband's right and opposite her daughter. George could see about two thirds of the judge's head over the daughter's. No problem making that shot.

Flicking the safety off, he lingered there, with his reticle centered on the judge's face.

The temptation to shoot was so strong, he almost did it.

But that would revenge, not justice.

George had thought it through thoroughly, and could not escape that fact. Killing the judge would be satisfying. Deeply satisfying. But it would not be justice.

Justice would be to inflict on her the wounds she had inflicted on him. And leave her without recourse, just as she had left him.

He said a quick prayer, asking God to explain what he was doing to Heather. Then he shifted the reticle from the judge to the back of the daughter's head.

He took a long, slow breath. Held it.

And squeezed the trigger.

Give A Dog A Dog A Bone

A Short Doggy Mystery

Michael Kingswood

Give A Dog A Bone

While on a run through a park with his best buddy John, Harry
the dog makes a grim discovery in the woods.

Harry loped along beside his best buddy John, the grass of the park where John liked to go running soft beneath Harry's feet and the air rife with scents: clipped grass, John's sweat, pollen, and despite the bright sun overhead, humidity like just before a good rain.

Breathing easily through his mouth and letting his tongue loll out to cool himself, Harry was content to just follow along beside John until he heard something moving off to the left, away from the path of dark stone that John seemed to like so much.

A new scent came to his nostrils then, and his lips drew back over his teeth as he recognized it. Rabbit.

Letting out a little yip, Harry surged forward and to the left, anticipation of a nice little snack bringing saliva to his mouth and setting his tail to wagging.

Then the thing around his neck dug in, and he came up short. He reared in the air, fighting against the restraint, but to no avail. It held fast, as John willed it.

"Harry, come back here," John said.

Harry looked back to see John had stopped running and was looking at him with an expression that Harry had learned meant he disapproved of what Harry had done, but was not angry.

Loping back to his buddy, Harry closed the distance between them, only a couple strides, and looked up at him.

John squatted down, the blue and white second skins on his legs and torso bunching up as he did so. "What'd you see over here?" he said, though the words just came across as playful and companionable sounds, and little more. Far more important than the sounds, John reached out with both hands and scratched at the area behind Harry's ears.

Harry shivered in delight—he loved when John did that—and his tail got to wagging more fervently, of its own accord.

Reaching up, he ran his tongue over the bottom half of John's face.

John leaned back and away, laughing, then straightened. He rubbed the top of Harry's head then said, "Come boy."

They ran some more, and Harry relished the feeling as his legs bunched and flexed and his toes dug into the dirt.

The stone path John followed continued through the field of grass and then passed beneath a cluster of weeping willows, though of course Harry didn't know the name for them. He always loved running beneath those tress because of the soft sound the dangling limbs and leaves made as they moved in the breeze, and because of the extensive shadow they cast. Harry wanted to just lie there and relax.

But John had other ideas, and the thing on Harry's neck urged him to keep up.

The willows were quickly forgotten, though, as the path bent to the left and the scent of water grew more strongly on the breeze.

The lake.

Harry loved the lake.

He sped up, but again the thing on his neck held him back, keeping him close to John. But it was all Harry could do not to burst, his anticipation had him tingling so.

The path rounded a small rise, and there is was: the lake.

If he'd known the word, pond would have been a more appropriate term. The body of water was not particularly broad, nor was it deep. But it had the most wonderful something in the center that sent water spewing skyward and then falling back down in a mass of sparkles that shimmered and reflected the sunlight in glints and sometimes mini-rainbows.

As he always did, John stopped for a rest at a strange almost-forest that stood at the side of the lake. It was a bunch of trees that weren't trees, logs without limbs and leaves clustered together at weird angles, with dull grey hard tubes connecting some of them together in some places, but not in others.

As Harry and John approached, there was another person at the weird forest. A female from the shape and scent of her, in tight-fitting yellow and white second skins. She was hanging from one of the hard tubes between logs. her arms bent double as she trembled to hold her chin up above the tube.

Strange. But John seemed to like that she was doing it.

There was a wooden bench—Harry knew what that was— not far from the strange forest. John dropped the end of the thing on Harry's neck atop one of the cross-pieces that made up the bench's back, so it was loosely looped over one of them, then stepped over toward where the female was hanging.

He said something as she dropped back to the ground, and she turned to face him. Her lips pulled back from her teeth as she saw him, and despite Harry having lived with humans for so long, he had to restrain his fighting reflexes for a second.

Bared teeth meant different with them, he always had to remind himself.

Harry settled down onto his haunches while John and the female exchanged noises, but Harry's attempt at becoming comfortable was interrupted by a high-pitched "Oh...so cute," from the female.

And then he was having his ears scratched again, and Harry couldn't complain.

He flicked his tongue into the female's face and she laughed, then stepped away from Harry and turned back to John.

Harry sniffed, and caught a faint odor from her that he had last scented a few moons ago, when John had brought a different female to their house and the two of them had begun wrestling together on the couch. The odor of that female's arousal had been so overpowering Harry had had to flee to a different room.

This one's was not so pungent. But it was there, and one man to another, he felt happy for John.

Then a fly buzzed past Harry's face, its wings almost striking his snout. Annoyed, Harry nipped at the air, but missed the bug.

It came back, and Harry tried again.

And again, no luck.

Harry sniffed and turned away from the annoying insect, which anyway had flown off to bother someone else. He paused when something else new came to his nostrils.

The breeze had shifted so it was now blowing toward the lake, through the woods on the other side of the stone path from the not-trees on the shore. And there was something…

Harry started forward, and found himself surprised when the thing on his neck didn't restrain him. He looked back and saw that the end of it had fallen from the bench and was now dragging behind him; it must have come off when he was jumping after the fly.

Back by the not-trees, John and the female were still making noises at each other. John would be fine there, Harry was sure.

He could go find out what this new thing was.

Harry padded across the black stone and beneath the canopy of the woods. The grass that had lined the path quickly gave way to bare dirt, and Harry felt his toes dig more deeply into the cool, slightly moist soil. It was comforting, in a way.

The leaves overhead rustled, and somewhere off to the right a bird made a high-pitched call that Harry didn't know.

And the odor grew stronger.

It was strange. Like some of the meats that John liked to grill or broil, but fundamentally different in some way Harry couldn't put his nose on.

And rotten, of course. But that wasn't the strangeness; he

had scented rotten before, and could pick out the various meats despite their rot, no problem.

But not this one.

He put his snout to the ground and ranged forward, moving left and right as he went further into the woods.

The scent was everywhere. But it seemed to be strongest coming from right…over…

Harry stopped in an area where the soil seemed somehow softer than elsewhere. He sniffed; whatever that meat was, it was here.

Time to dig.

Harry lolled his tongue out, happiness washing over him. He loved to dig, too.

The soil *was* more loose here, and more damp as well. Little shivers of contentment flowed up Harry's legs as his toes dug into the moist coolness beneath, and loosed greater nose-fulls of the strangely enticing, yet also somehow abhorrent, odor beneath.

"Harry!"

His name—not his true name but the one John had given him—rang through the air, but Harry paid the call no heed. Faster he dug, his toes unearthing hidden treasures that any other day he would have investigated for hours. Today, though, he only had nose for whatever it was that had created the odor that drew him on.

Deeper he went, and deeper still, and still it eluded him.

Another voice, higher-pitched, joined in with John's, calling out to him. "Harry!"

Part of Harry's mind grinned in triumph for his best buddy, for he had clearly secured himself a mate this day.

But that didn't matter, because what was causing that scent?

"There you are!" It was John's voice, near behind him.

And there it was. The last few pawfulls of dirt had

unearthed it, and now it lay beneath him. It was decaying, but there was enough of it left to see it for what it was. It was rotting, but there was enough unturned meat to make its scent almost appealing.

Except that it resembled his best buddy so much he would never dream of sinking his teeth into it.

"What is he getting into?" said the higher, female voice.

"No idea," said John, and then the thing on Harry's neck tightened, and strong arms pulled him back. "Come on, boy, get out of - "

John's voice broke, his sounds halting in a gurgle of surprise and shock.

The female made an, "Oh!" that was all fear mixed with revulsion.

John pulled Harry the rest of the way out of the hole Harry had made, and Harry only resisted a little bit. Because now he realized what it was he was looking at; an appendage just like his best buddy's, except it was detached from the body of the human who used to own it.

"Call 911," John said, and he swallowed hard.

The meaning of his sounds escaped Harry, but the sense of horror, of revulsion, with which he made them did not.

THE SUN WAS ALMOST GONE BEHIND the trees, and still they remained there in the not-forest of not-trees next to the lake.

Many more humans had come, strangely dressed in dark blue second-skins, with dark blue things atop their heads and a sense of officialness that implied a whole other skin that was invisible, but also undeniably there.

They had brought with them great noisy transports, like John's except larger, that had torn up the ground around the lake as they charged into the area and that flashed brilliant lights into the growing shadows of the fleeing day. White, Blue, and Red, they dazzled Harry's eyes every time he looked their way. So he stopped doing so, instead looking away from them toward the waters and the strangely comforting thing that spat upward in the center of the lake.

The official humans made noises at John again and again, and at his new mate. But eventually they let her go. She and John made noises to each other, and he did something with a flat black thing he always kept in a pouch of his second skin. Then she left, moving quickly past the flashing transports in the direction of a place Harry could vaguely recall.

Wasn't it in that direction that he and John had originally come from? Where John had left his own transport thing, so similar yet so much less disturbing than those that the official humans used?

Harry supposed it didn't really matter.

In the time—he had only a vague notion of time, just that things moved on from where they were, becoming something else but without notion of a goal to that becoming—Harry and John had waited there, other official humans, dressed less martially but possessing the same air of being about stern business, had cordoned off the woods where Harry had made his discovery.

Much to his disdain. Twice he had managed to loosen the thing on his neck and tried to go back there. And twice he had been intercepted and prevented from doing so.

Harry bared his teeth and growled at the last human who had stopped him and delivered him back to John, and the official human with him. How to make him understand Harry didn't want to eat the things under the trees?

He would never do that. Too much like his best buddy.

But he did want to know what they were, and how they got there.

It didn't matter; he never got the chance to look again. Not long after that second attempt, the official human with John clasped forearms with him, then turned his back on Harry's best buddy.

A breath later, John said, "Let's go, boy," and the thing on Harry's neck urged him into motion.

He walked next to John as John headed in the same direction the female had gone, some time earlier. Toward his transport, and then, Harry presumed, back home.

Drat it. If they went home he'd never be able to figure out -

He hadn't noticed until right this moment that in addition to the official humans, others had gathered around the lake. Humans of all shades, wearing all sorts of second skins, were watching the goings on with the official ones, and in the woods.

They smelled of curiosity and good humor. A few of dread. And one…

As he and John drew near to the one human who stood apart from the others, garbed in a single grey second skin, Harry's hackles rose.

The human's scent was mostly normal: sweat and the strange aromatic thing that they used to conceal their sweat. But beneath that, mostly emanating from the skin he had slung over his shoulder, came another scent that was both alluring and abhorrent.

A scent that Harry recognized from the woods over by the lake.

Harry bared his teeth and growled, and he surged forward toward the strange human.

"Harry - " John sounded surprised, and the thing on Harry's neck tightened for a second, then let go as Harry heard John fall behind him.

The strangely-scented human's eyes widened as Harry leapt onto him, and he collapsed onto the ground.

The skin that he had slung over his shoulder fell as well, landing on the ground a pace away.

Paying the human no further mind, Harry dove at the skin and began tearing at it.

"What the - ?"

"Help him!"

"Damn dog!"

"Harry!"

A multitude of voices rose from all around, but Harry paid them no heed. He bit at the skin, tearing at it... And then it opened, and its contents fell out.

Immediately, the mood among the surrounding humans shifted. From anger at Harry, they now smelled of revulsion, or horror.

Of anger.

And, from the one Harry had knocked over, of fear.

That human tried to scramble to his feet and run, but others surged forward and knocked him down.

"Don't move! You're under arrest!"

Official voices took over, but Harry only heard John's as he knelt down beside him.

"Easy boy," John said, but only the comforting tone carried meaning. "Come on."

The thing around his neck didn't need to pull him away from the skin on the ground. John's arms did that for him.

BACK AT HOME, and Harry raced ahead of John across the entryway and into his room, with its big couch and chairs, and his bed over in the corner.

He found his little round toy and leapt on it, biting and pressing down, then feeling a surge of supreme joy when it emitted its little high-pitched squeak.

Harry shook his head, thrashing the toy about, then tossed it aside and watched it bounce across the room.

Then he bounded forward to bite at it again.

Heard but unnoticed behind him, John was talking into his black thing as he followed Harry into the room.

" - must have been cutting his victims up and bringing the pieces to the park one by one."

A pause, which Harry barely registered as the toy's squeak rang out again. Then John shrugged.

"Cops told me sometimes these sickos like to hang around the crime scene. Gives them a feeling of power, to watch people's reaction to their work."

The toy bounced away, but Harry cast it from his mind. He had come near to his water bowl, and its odor reminded him of his need for drink.

He bent his head over and began lapping up the cool fluid.

"Yeah, I got her number. We're going out tomorrow night." John laughed. "We'll see. Later man."

Then he set the black thing down on the flat wooden thing that dominated the room.

Harry saw this from the corner of his eye but didn't pay any heed until John came over and squatted down next to him. He was carrying another skin in his hands.

"I've got something for you, boy," John said. Then his hands made some indecipherable movements with the skin he was holding.

A scent come straight from heaven issued forth as the skin opened, and Harry pulled his head up out of the water bowl. Was that - ?

It was.

John pulled a great big bone out of the skin. And not just a bone. It had meat on it.

Cow meat.

John held the bone out, and for a moment Harry could do nothing but just look at it, saliva flooding into his mouth as he took in the bounty before him.

Was this real?

"Come get it, boy," John said, and he wiggled the bone around in the air.

That was all the encouragement Harry needed. He thrust his head forward and closed his teeth around the proferred treat.

Cow meat and blood and salt and marrow and thousands other flavors at once struck Harry's tongue, and it was all he could do not to swoon on the spot. But he was made of sterner stuff than that.

Mostly.

Moving quickly lest he tempt fate into taking the bounty away, he hurried over to his bed, circled once, and lied down, bone and meat in front of him between his forepaws.

Then he began gnawing. And he did not intend to stop until every last bit of this tasty morsel was gone, though it take him a week.

He had no notion of what a week was; or even what a day or a year truly was. But what notion of time's passage he did have, he projected out to an equivalent length.

Or not. Whatever thought of time, or its meaning, fled before the flavors cascading through his tongue and into his body. He just chewed and chewed and chewed.

So captivated was he that he almost missed the comparatively small pleasure of John scratching him behind the ears and saying, "Good boy."

Almost.

Bag Man

A Sexy And Deadly Short Mystery

Michael Kingswood

Bag Man

A mysterious bag that everyone wants. An employer who is as dangerous as she is beautiful. A man on the run.

It was supposed to be a routine pickup, just another day on the job.

If only it had been that easy.

Pain flared from the wound in Jayme's abdomen, pulsing in time with the lifeblood spurting from the cut. He gritted his teeth to keep from crying out, but a guttural groan still issued from his lips. Though he knew it was futile, he nevertheless pressed his hands against the wound, trying in vain to stem the flow of blood and to preserve his life.

"I can't believe that bitch pulled a knife on me."

In spite of himself, Jayme laughed at his partner's remark, though doing so caused the pain to intensify, turning his guffaw into another groan that was almost, but not quite, a scream.

Beside him on the floor, Rolf also lay wounded, though he was not nearly in as bad a state. His left arm hung limply, his shoulder dislocated at least, and he had a deep cut in his right thigh. But, unlike Jayme, he would clearly live through the day unless something drastic happened.

The bastard.

Of course, it looked like something drastic was about to happen. Jayme turned his head to see Ismerelda stepping through the front door, along with her two guards. Had he been healthy, Jayme would have disregarded the guards out of hand; they were brainless thugs who knew only brute force, not subtlety. But in his current state…

With a rueful smile, Jayme drew in a breath and spoke. Or rather, he tried to, but all that came out was a rattling grunt, itself almost a groan. He swallowed, the act itself all but useless considering his mouth was dry as a desert. But it worked, for when he tried to speak again, words actually came forth.

"She…cut your leg," he said. "You *shot* me."

Rolf actually looked embarrassed. "Yeah, well," he said, "sorry 'bout that. Wasn't my fault. Just business, right?"

Right. Just business.

THE DAY STARTED out promisingly enough.

Jayme and Rolf were on assignment. They met at 10:30 and drove to their meet in the back room at Fabricio's, a small coffee shop in a strip mall not far from the airport that was owned by a guy who was friendly with Jayme's employers. For a little kickback each month, he looked the other way at some of the business deals that went down there. It was a convenient setup, especially since Fabricio made some of the best crepes in town, and great coffee to go with them.

They were supposed to meet up with a man from Puerto Rico about a bag. They were to know him by the black fedora he liked to wear. Simple enough; they had done similar jobs countless times. Except when they showed up at the meet, there was no man present who met that description.

There was, however, an extremely attractive woman in a tight-fitting blue dress. Tall - maybe five foot ten, without her high heels - and with a body that any red-blooded man would die for, it was easy to miss looking at her face. Which would be a mistake because she had the deepest blue eyes Jayme had ever seen, lips of deep red, and a heart-shaped face that would stand out in any beauty pageant, all framed by hair so blond it was almost white.

He should have known it was a set-up.

They waited for fifteen minutes, and spent most of the time staring at the woman as they sipped a couple cups of coffee. She sat at a table in the corner by herself, sipping a cup of tea, reading the paper, and pretending not to notice their stares. Finally, Jayme decided the meet was blown and nudged Rolf, who nodded reluctantly and stood along with Jayme. They only made a single step toward the door before the thugs stepped inside.

They were not particularly tall, but broad and muscular, with similar enough bodies and faces that Jayme assumed they were brothers. They wore suits that were neither cheap nor expensive and simple black sunglasses. Their suit coats bulged ever so slightly on their left sides beneath their armpits. An untrained eye would not even notice it, but Jayme was not untrained. They were packing heat and, from the look of them, they probably would not hesitate for long in using it.

"Why don't you gentlemen sit down," a sultry voice spoke from behind them.

Jayme and Rolf exchanged glances. Rolf shrugged and turned around, and Jayme followed him over to the woman's table.

She had set the paper down and was staring at them with a little smile on her lips, the kind of smile that said she knew secrets they would kill to learn. As they approached, the woman picked up her tea cup again and gestured with her free hand toward the chairs across from herself as she took another sip.

There was nothing to do but sit down and see where this was going, so Jayme hesitated only a heartbeat before unbuttoning his sports coat and taking one of the two chairs. Rolf settled in as well, looking more casual in his jeans and leather jacket - Jayme had never been able to get him to dress the part better - and the waiting game began.

In tense situations like the one Jayme found himself in that morning, some people seemed to find it amusing to wait, as though a few moments of silence would make him squirm. He supposed maybe your everyday Joe on the street would find that silence uncomfortable, especially with a couple of armed thugs at his back. But Jayme had long since learned that there can be great advantage in speaking second and besides, he hated playing stupid games. So he sat still and stared at the woman for a long few moments, drinking in the sight of her while he waited. It was far from the most unpleasant staredown he had ever participated in.

The woman's smile broadened slightly and she sniffed, then

set her teacup down. "I'm afraid your contact won't be making an appearance this morning," she said in the same sultry voice that she used to 'invite' them over.

"Not sure what you're talking about, miss," Rolf replied with aplomb. "We're just here for coffee."

She sniffed dismissively and shot Rolf an annoyed look. "Please," she said, her tone scornful. "I think we can skip the games and get right to the point, don't you?"

Jayme and Rolf traded another glance. Rolf looked almost apologetic as he shrugged slightly in the manner that said he would let Jayme take the lead.

"Fair enough," Jayme said. "I assume you know where he is, miss…" He let the sentence trail away into a question.

"You may call me Ismerelda. And yes, I do."

Jayme leaned back in his chair and sighed. "And I suppose you're not going to tell us." He hated when this sort of thing happened.

Ismerelda surprised him, though. Her smile grew and she shook her head. "Oh I am absolutely going to tell you." She traced one finger along the rim of her teacup, making a soft humming sound despite it not being made of crystal. "But I want something in return."

This was getting tiresome. "Look lady," Jayme said, "I don't have time for this." Pressing his palms against the tabletop, Jayme moved to stand up. The sound of two hammers being pulled back behind him made him stop.

Ismerelda tsk'd softly. "Mr. Hawthorn, I think you and Mr. Steinman really want to hear what I have to say."

That got Jayme's attention, and he slowly lowered himself back into his chair. How had she known his name? From the corner of his eye, Jayme saw that Rolf was thinking similarly, and that her knowledge took him off guard. Shoving sudden doubt away, Jayme put his poker face on and twirled his index finger in the air in a 'get on with it' motion.

Ismerelda's eyebrows quirked upward slightly as Jayme's gesture, but if it irked her she did not let it show in her tone of voice. "I want the bag."

Jayme was so stunned he laughed before he could stop himself. The utter gall of this broad!

He got himself under control after a few seconds, but he could see his laughter had annoyed her in a way his gesture had not. The smile vanished from her face, replaced by a tight little scowl, and her brow furrowed as she narrowed her eyes at him.

"That was not a joke, Mr. Hawthorn."

Jayme snorted and leaned forward. "It sounded like one to me. That bag belongs to someone else, and it's my job to get it to him. I don't know who you think you are, but if you think I'm just going to renege on a contract because you say so, you've got another thing coming."

Ismerelda surprised him again. "It does belong to someone, Mr. Hawthorn. Me."

"You?"

She nodded. "The courier you were to meet stole it from my business associate. It's contents are quite valuable to me, and I want them back."

That did not make any sense. "Why don't you just take it back then? If you know where he is…"

"The situation is…complicated. If I take a direct hand in this, it may upset some very carefully laid plans, and I don't want that to happen."

"So just send other goons. We have people we work for, too, and they spent good money for that bag. They won't appreciate it if we just blow them off to help you."

Ismerelda smiled again, that teasing smile that made him question his assumptions. Slowly, ever so slowly, she lifted a small handbag, barely more than a pouch really, up onto the table from the seat next to her. The bag was held shut by a small clasp at its top, which she flipped open with a casual flick of her fingers.

"I don't think they will mind."

As she spoke, she withdrew a small stack of photographs, old-school polaroids from the look of them, and tossed them onto the table.

Jayme glanced down at the photos and had to stop himself from gasping in shocked surprise. Rolf failed to do the same. Each photograph showed a dead man, shot through the temple with a small caliber bullet. Jayme recognized all of them.

"As you can see," Ismerelda went on, "your employers no longer care about my bag." Resting her elbows on the table, she folded her hands together and rested her chin upon them. She would have been cute enough to kiss right then, except for her demonstrated ruthlessness. How the hell…

"How the hell did *you* get to *them*?" Rolf said, echoing Jayme's thoughts.

Ismerelda smirked. "A girl needs her secrets, Mr. Steinman." Her gaze flittered between them for a moment before settling back onto Jayme. "Since you are independent contractors now, it would be in your interest to help me. It is better than the alternative." Her eyes flicked down toward the photos again.

No mistaking that threat. Crap.

"What's our cut?"

"Ten grand. Each. And I'll make a point of mentioning how professional you are to my friends, should they need assistance later." Her smile was almost mocking now.

"Riiiight." Jayme looked at Rolf.

The other man wore a deep frown, but when he met Jayme's gaze, he shrugged. The shrug spoke volumes.

Jayme had to admit, he had a point. What were they supposed to do, get killed from loyalty to their old bosses? He snorted inwardly; he had not liked them, and certainly only respected the paychecks they handed out. As far as Jayme was concerned, they got what they deserved.

So what the hell, a bird in the hand, and all that.

"Ok, you've got a deal."

"Excellent."

In retrospect, it was not his smartest move ever.

SINCE THEIR ORIGINAL contact was coming from Puerto Rico, most people who wanted to track him down would have looked for him in hotels close to the airport. He picked one far away.

Smart. Professionally smart.

The Indigo Motel sat on a frontage road that ran alongside the Interstate, about twenty miles from the airport. It was old, probably built in the 50s, and was badly in need of a paint job and remodeling. It was the sort of place that probably was not very particular about its clientele.

Jayme drove his Mustang past the motel and scoped out the area. There were five other cars visible, all non-descript late-model sedans of various makes. None would particularly stand out, and any could be their man's vehicle.

"Room twenty-five, right there." Rolf pointed at the door in question as they rolled past and narrowed his eyes, studying it intently. "Curtains are drawn. Can't tell if he's in there."

The parking spot in front of the room was empty, but that did not mean anything. A pro would park elsewhere, maybe, to throw off the scent.

"Let's circle back in a few minutes," Jayme said, and got a nod of agreement from Rolf.

They stopped for a short while at a gas station a couple miles away to top off the tank and use the facilities. Then they reversed course.

A new car was parked in the Motel lot, a yellow Mazda

coup that stood out like a sore thumb among all the other vehicles there. As they drove past, Jayme saw a woman step out of the driver's side door and take a look around.

She was average height, dressed simply in jeans and a loose t-shirt, and sunglasses. She had strawberry blonde hair that was pulled back from her eyes and tied in a small bun on the back of her head, like a military woman who does not want a short haircut will do. Jayme would not have looked at her twice, except she went up to Room Twenty-Five and knocked on the door.

"Well, well," Jayme said as they left the motel behind. "Our man's got company."

"Didn't look like a hooker."

Jayme snorted. "It's a little early in the day for that."

Rolf chuckled. "Not really. You can find a working girl twenty-four hours a day, if you know where to look."

Jayme rolled his eyes. Rolf was sometimes a bit crass. "Whatever."

They parked in a lot a few hundred yards away from the motel and settled in to wait. There were still several hours of daylight remaining, and it would be better to do the job while the guy was alone, anyway.

Turns out, they did not have to wait long.

Maybe ten minutes later, the door to room twenty-five opened and the woman stepped back out into the sunlight.

"That was quick," Rolf said, and smirked.

Always in the gutter, he was. Jayme rolled his eyes again, then returned his attention to their quarry.

The woman got into her car, but did not drive off immediately. What was she waiting for?

Then a man emerged from the room. He was thin, a bit taller than average, and wore a dark business suit. He paused for a moment just outside his door to don a fedora, then walked over to the woman's car and got into the passenger seat, pausing only to shove the bulky duffle bag he carried into the back seat.

Jayme leaned forward, his eyes narrowing. The duffle bag.

"Looks like he had another meet set up besides ours," Rolf said.

Jayme nodded slowly. It almost made sense; the man probably would have wanted to shop the bag around, get the best price. But the meet was all set up. He would not want to piss off the kinds of people Jayme and Rolf worked for, not over a few bucks. Unless…

"Motherfucker," he said, sudden anger making him grip the steering wheel tightly enough that his knuckles turned white.

Rolf glanced at him questioningly. He did not see it.

"That fucker knew Ismerelda was after him, so he set up the meet with us as a diversion. He's been playing us from the start."

Rolf's sudden scowl likely matched Jayme's own. "Let's get him."

The Mazda pulled out of the Motel parking lot and turned left. It passed Jayme and Rolf's position, and Jayme got a good look in the windows for a moment. The woman was laughing about something.

Jayme started his Mustang back up and put it in gear. Time to do the job.

The Mazda got onto the Interstate and drove west for forty-five minutes, well past the outskirts of suburbia and into the boonies, then turned off onto a two-lane country road. Jayme followed at a discreet distance, being careful to keep one or two cars between himself and the Mazda; he did not want to spook the game too early.

The country road twisted and turned through sprawling woods and around several small hills, and Jayme lost sight of the other car on more than one occasion. But always it was there again when he rounded the bend.

Until suddenly it was not.

He checked the rearview mirror.

Nothing.

He looked to either side.

Nothing. What the hell?

"Maybe they sped up." From the tone of his voice, Rolf did not believe that any more than Jayme did. The pair in the Mazda had given them the slip. But where?

A half-mile up the road was a small turnoff. Jayme used it to make a three-point turn, then drove back the way he came, more slowly than before.

He saw it this time. Halfway through the turn, a small dirt trail, mostly hidden from view by large bushes until he was right on it, led away from the road to the right.

Jayme stopped the Mustang and looked down the trail. It curved to the left about a hundred yards down; the trees obscured everything beyond that. But there were fresh tire marks.

They had to have come this way; there was nowhere else for them to go.

He and Rolf exchanged looks. Rolf, looking grim, reached beneath his leather jacket and unsnapped the tab holding his Beretta into its shoulder holster.

Jayme's Sig was nestled into a holster at the small of his back; it would be hard to draw in a hurry while he was sitting down. He took a moment to pull it out and check he had remembered to chamber a round earlier. Then he tucked it into the space between his seat and the center console and turned off onto the dirt trail.

He drove slowly, but it made no difference. The Mustang

was not designed for smooth travel off of pavement. It jounced all over the place, bumping and swaying. Before they reached the bend to the left, Rolf was already holding onto the hand grip on the door and looking a bit green; he got motion sickness from the strangest things.

Not that Jayme liked the ride any more than he did. The constant bumping began to do a number on his back; it ached some days, and the bumping did not help matters.

They rounded the bend, then a second that turned to the right. The trees began to thin ahead as the trail approached yet another turn to the left. Jayme could just make out a small two-story cabin through the trees in that direction.

He applied the brakes, stopping the Mustang.

It would not do to drive right up to the building. Their man and his lady would be watching for that, and even if they were dumb enough not to be - Jayme rather doubted that - driving up would make noise and draw their attention.

Jayme looked around for a moment, then turned the Mustang to the right and, moving very slowly, slipped it off to the side of the trail, where the trees offered a few feet of clearance. Not that he expected anyone else to drive up here. But he did not like the notion of blocking the only road out of there, just in case.

Shutting off the car's engine, Jayme pulled his Sig out and took a deep breath. Then he nodded to Rolf and opened the car door.

JAYME CREPT up to the cabin's back door while Rolf approached a window a few feet to the right. It was quiet. He could almost believe there was no one inside, except for the Mazda parked out front and the smoke wisping out of the chimney.

They were in there, all right.

He reached the door and slowly tried the knob. It turned freely in his hand; unlocked.

A glance over at Rolf, long enough to see the other man's nod, told him all he needed to know. The coast was clear, at least in the rear of the house.

Slowly, carefully, he pulled the door open. It moved smoothly on its hinges, making barely a sound. That was a relief; Jayme had been screwed by squeaking hinges a couple times. But not this time. It was all starting to come together.

He smiled thinly and stepped inside, Rolf close behind.

The back room was a kitchen. Small, with appliances that dated from the 60s probably, it nevertheless was a pleasant place. The scent of baked bread lingered in the air, making Jayme's mouth water. The lady of the house was handy with the oven, it seemed. His kind of girl.

Jayme moved carefully, on the balls of his feet to minimize his noise, to the doorway leading deeper into the house. Sig held up beside his face, he stopped at the edge of the doorway and eased his head forward so he could peek around.

The next room was a combination dining room and living room - some folks call those great rooms, said the part of his mind that he usually turned off in these circumstances. The furniture was dated, just like the kitchen, but everything was tidy and arranged just so. Off to the left, near the cabin's front door, a set of stairs led to the upper level, probably where the bedrooms were located.

A woman, the woman from the car, stood with her back to Jayme, looking out the front window.

She was naked.

Jayme did a double-take.

She was still naked. And Lord, did she have a great ass.

Jayme swallowed and flexed his fingers around the grip of his Sig. Trying not to think about the view in front of him, he glanced back over his shoulder toward Rolf and pointed the first two fingers of his left hand toward his eyes, then held up his index finger. *I see one person.*

Rolf nodded. *Let's do it.*

Jayme took a deep breath then looked back around the corner again.

She was still there. Still naked. But she was now facing the kitchen, and for a moment, he enjoyed the full frontal view. Her ass had nothing on her front. Glory be!

Their eyes met, and hers widened in surprised shock. No time to stop and admire the view.

Jayme lowered his Sig and stepped fully into the room, painfully aware of the fact that he was about the burst his pants from the hard-on he was growing. He did his best to ignore it, though, as he sighted the weapon in on her, center of mass.

"Don't move," he ordered in his coldest, most business-like tone.

Rolf bolted around the corner a second later, his Beretta held at the ready. He stopped abruptly upon seeing the woman.

"Holy shit," he said breathlessly.

For a moment, they stood there, the two of them with their weapons trained on the woman. She frozen in mid-movement, her eyes flickering between their faces, then lowering as she no doubt noticed the effect she was having on them.

Jayme cursed nature right then. How could you make a woman believe you were going to blow her away when your body told her you really wanted *her* to blow *you?*

Her lips curled upward slightly. She knew her advantage, despite their having the drop on her.

Shit.

A single gunshot, from off to the left, broke the spell.

THE BULLET WHIZZED past Jayme's head and he felt his hair ruffle from the wake it left in the air.

That was *way* too close.

Pivoting on his heel, Jayme saw his man.

He stood halfway down the staircase from the second level, dressed only in his boxer shorts. He was ready for his lady, but that tent was quickly lowering. In his hands was a fair-sized revolver, probably a .357, but from the awkward way he was recovering from the gun's recoil, he did not shoot very often, at least not with a weapon of that caliber.

He had a wild look in his eyes, as though he was scared out of his wits.

Jayme did not pause to consider why the guy had carried a gun down from upstairs if he was planning to bang his girl-friend, or whatever she was. He just dropped to one knee, sighted in, and fired before the guy could recover enough from the revolver's recoil to fire again.

Jayme's round struck the man in the shoulder. He pinwheeled around into the wall, then lost his balance and tumbled down the staircase to the landing before the front door.

From behind him, Rolf shouted an oath that became a cry of pain.

Jayme spun back around and saw the woman, still naked but clutching a knife like a trained fighter, pull back from Rolf as he stumbled forward. Her blade dripped red spots onto the floor, and Jayme could see a corresponding cut on his partner's thigh.

Rolf fell to his knee, but managed to stabilize himself before hitting the ground completely.

The woman noticed Jayme turning back toward her and crouched, then spun around behind Rolf. It was going to be hard to shoot her without hitting him, but Jayme brought his Sig to bear, looking for his shot.

Rolf ruined it. He tried to turn his weapon on the woman as well, but she continued to move.

She was fast, much faster than Jayme would have thought. One moment she was behind Rolf as he turned toward her, the next, she was at his side, his left arm - he was a lefty - in a lock that made him arch his back and grimace in pain...and point his gun directly at Jayme.

The woman smiled and gave a little jerk of her shoulders, and Rolf cried out again. Jayme could only watch in shock as his partner's finger clenched on the trigger in reaction.

The round hit Jayme dead center in the gut, crumpling him over and sending him to the ground before he realized what had happened.

Then the pain hit, and it was all he could do to hold back a scream.

He tried to raise his gun before she finished him, but there was no time.

The woman wrenched Rolf's arm again, and his hand went limp, dropping his Beretta into her hand. Then she kicked his good leg out from under him and turned fully toward Jayme, taking careful aim at him.

"Lose the gun," she ordered, her voice cool and calm.

Jayme was impressed to see that she had not broken a sweat, and was not even breathing heavily. But then, that she was in great shape was obvious just from looking at her. She was a sight to see, for certain. But just then, Jayme was not surprised to realize he was not that interested.

Slowly, he raised his gun hand - he feared what would happen with his belly if he took his other hand from the wound - and tossed the Sig off to the side.

Then he waited for the kill shot.

She did not fire. Instead, her eyes flickered past Jayme toward the man at the bottom of the stairs.

"You ok, baby?"

A low groan was his initial reply, but then he managed, "It hurts like a bitch!" It sounded like he was clenching his teeth.

"Get up. We have to go."

"Babe, I…"

"*Now*!"

Jayme heard the man struggling to his feet, but never took his eyes off the woman.

She licked her lips and stepped away from him and Rolf, toward the couch where, Jayme could see now, her clothing lay haphazardly. Taking one hand off the gun, she scooped up the garments and pressed them against her side to hold them tight. Her aim remained steady the whole time.

"Get the bag and let's get out of here."

The man whimpered, but Jayme heard him slowly maneuver upstairs. A few moments later, he came back down. From the sound of it, he almost fell down the stairs twice.

The woman circled around toward the door. Jayme followed her with her eyes. Against his better judgment, hope blossomed within him. If she was going to finish them off, she would have done it by now. Wouldn't she?

At the door, she looked away from Jayme long enough to give her man a quick once-over. Then she jerked her head toward the door. While the man stepped outside, she returned her gaze to Jayme and Rolf.

"Don't follow us. You won't get off this easy next time." She spoke with such a confident assurance that, even had he not witnessed her prowess first hand a moment before, Jayme would have believed her.

Then she stepped through the door and out of sight.

Two gunshots rang out from the front of the house.

A moment later, Jayme saw Ismerelda through the open door.

Ismerelda stopped a few feet away from Jayme and Rolf. She wore a disapproving expression as she looked down at them.

"Gentlemen," she said. "That did not go as well as I would have hoped."

Jayme managed a half-shrug. Or at least he tried to, but moving even that much sent a new wave of pain through his belly.

Rolf did the talking this time. "How the hell did *you* get here?"

"My man planted a GPS tracker on your car while we spoke earlier." She looked around the room and pursed her lips. "Sloppy. Very sloppy."

Rolf glowered at her. "You could have warned us he was meeting a ninja."

Ismerelda quirked an eyebrow upward at his words. "You could have done a better job researching your target before you went in with guns blazing." She shook her head, then gestured with her left hand.

The guard on that side stepped forward and reached inside his suit coat. Jayme cringed, but when the man's hand came back out, it held an envelope, not a gun.

Ismerelda took the proffered envelope and flicked it open. After a quick check of its contents, she nodded quickly, then tossed it onto the floor.

"Your money," she said, by way of explanation. "We will not meet again."

Then she turned away from them. The guards exited the room and she made to follow. But she paused before stepping through the door, looking back at Jayme with icy eyes.

"I took the liberty of calling for assistance. Ambulances are on the way, if you wish to wait for them." She smiled then, a smile that was just as cold as her eyes. "I expect the Police will be along as well. Good luck!"

And then she was gone.

"Ah fuck," Rolf said. He forced himself to his feet, grimacing. "We gotta get out of here."

Rolf limped over to the envelope and picked it up, grunting with every movement. Stuffing the money in his pocket, he turned to Jayme and offered his right hand.

Somehow they managed to get Jayme up on his feet. Then they set off toward the door, and the Mustang. Jayme had to lean on Rolf's shoulder for support. It was excruciating, but he really did not want to be there when the cops showed up.

"You got the car keys?"

Jayme nodded and fumbled into his pocket for them.

They made it as far as the door. Then Jayme's legs buckled, and Rolf could not stop him from falling again.

He hit the floor and cried out as renewed pain flared out of the wound. Vaguely, he heard the keys strike the floor a couple feet away, but his entire world was pain for a long minute and he paid it no mind.

When he managed to resolve anything besides the pain of his wound, Rolf was standing over him, the car keys clutched in his right hand. From the bulge under his arm, his Beretta was back in its shoulder holster; he must have retrieved it from the woman's corpse outside.

Rolf met Jayme's gaze in silence for a long moment. In addition to the pain in his belly, Jayme began to get a cold feeling in the pit of his stomach from the look on the other man's face.

"This isn't going to work, partner," Rolf said.

"No. Rolf, we can…"

"No time. Hear that?"

Sure enough, now that Rolf mentioned it, Jayme *could* hear it. Faint, but getting slowly louder.

Sirens.

"Been good working with you, brother."

And then Rolf turned and limped down the front porch

and toward the Mustang, back where they left it on the trail leading to the house.

As he heard the car start and saw the rising dust as Rolf sped away, Jayme collapsed back onto the floor, his breath coming in quick pants. He listened to the sirens growing louder and found, however much he wanted to, that he could not curse Rolf for leaving him to the Cops.

After all, it was just business.

Fresh Out
A Short Crime Story

Michael Kingswood

Fresh Out

Newly released after fifteen years in prison, Bill seeks to restart his life, and get revenge on the woman who framed him.

Bill couldn't get used to how his clothes felt. After fifteen years of wearing nothing but prison coveralls, the jeans and red, long-sleeved collard shirt he had on when he was booked seemed like someone's else's attire.

And here, sitting in the passenger seat of Joey's car, he kept expecting to hear a guard shouting his name, ripping him a new one for not being dressed right.

He watched the streetlights that lined the highway leading down toward Norfolk pass on either side, and could not shake that feeling. Or the little panicky feeling that threatened to jump up through his chest at the expansive world out there, a world without walls or fences that he was now able to experience, once again.

Inside, he'd scoffed at guys who talked about people they knew who couldn't hack it out in the world and who had gotten busted just so they could come back to the clink, to the world they knew and understood. What kind of moronic pussy would do something like that?

But now, looking out at it for the first time in so long, Bill understood.

"Feels good, don't it."

From behind the wheel, Joey looked over at Bill and grinned. He was Bill's age, mid-40s, with curly black hair that was flecked with grey strands here and there, dark eyes, and a handsome oval face and ready grin that always attracted the ladies. He had done well for himself while Bill was inside, to all appearances. He drove a Dodge Charger with all the trimmings, and wore a stylish black leather jacket over a white shirt that Bill was pretty sure was silk. He was surrounded by the subtle musk of expensive cologne, and his watch glittered silver; probably cost a few grand. If that weren't enough, he'd had his left incisor capped with gold.

Doing ok.

Bill shrugged, and Joey chuckled.

"It takes a little getting used to. I wasn't in as long as you, but I know. Believe me."

Joey had done three years for dealing, back before he got smart about things. He was mostly straight now, or at least had been back before Bill went away. Pretty much the exact opposite route Bill had taken, come to think on it.

But then, Joey had actually done what he was put away for. Bill couldn't relate to that.

They turned off at the exit to Hampton, and Bill raised an eyebrow Joey's way. "You don't live in Chesapeake anymore?"

Joey shrugged as he eased the car into its new lane. "After Lisa left, I - " He broke off when he saw Bill's expression. "Shit. Sorry, forgot you didn't know." He sighed and shook his head. "She kicked me to the curb two years ago. Got it in her head that she's destined to be a movie star. Took Kevin, and split to LA."

"No shit?"

Joey shrugged again. "Chicks, man. What're you gonna do?"

Which was one thing, but Lisa had taken Joey's son with her. If a girl had done that to Bill…

But then, Rachel had done that to him, hadn't she? Worse, actually. She'd set it up so he would take the fall for her caper, and then he went to rot in prison where he hadn't seen his son in fifteen years. While she was probably living the high life and banging quarterbacks, or something.

He was going to need dental surgery if he didn't stop grinding his teeth. He focused back on Joey. "Sorry, man."

Joey grinned at him. "Not your fault, brother."

He turned left, and they departed the main road for a quieter residential street. It was one of those streets where the trees planted on either side reached out and covered the road with their branches, with houses that were not McMansions but still respectably big and constructed with that distinctly southern front porch that's begging for a swing where a father could sit to clean his shotgun while his daughter was off on her first date.

Halfway down the block, Joey turned left into the driveway of a single-story house that, of course, had the required porch. A pair of lamps that flickered like torches lit the stairs leading up to the porch and the front door. The place was lit as though occupied already.

He looked sidelong at Joey. "You're not throwing me a party, are you?"

Joey sniffed and shut off the engine. "Nothing major," he said, and grinned at him.

Bill followed Joey up the stairs to his house and could not shake off a sense of trepidation. The absolute last thing he wanted to do right now was deal with people. Really, he just wanted to get settled, have a beer, then hit the rack. He had a lot to do, and the sooner he got about it, the better.

Bill's house was spacious, but not enormous. The door opened into a great room that spanned most of the house's width. Deep blue paint on the walls balanced the off-white tiles that made up the flooring. A simply elegant dining set with seating for six lay off to the right. Directly in front of the door, a black leather sectional couch faced a flat screen that was wider than Bill was tall. The kitchen was in the rear right portion of the room, with white cabinets and a dark grey stone countertop bar splitting the appliances from the living and dining areas. Two closed doors stood off to Bill's left, and a hallway just to the right of the flat screen lead back deeper into the house. Muted jazz was playing as they walked in, and the place had a pleasant almost pinewood odor.

"Home sweet home," Joey said, spreading his hands to take in the space and grinning broadly. "You're in there," he pointed toward the second of the two doors to the left. "Got your own bathroom." He gestured toward the hallway. "I'm in back. Put your stuff down and get settled; I'll get you a drink."

That sounded real good, actually.

Bill went through the indicated door and found a decently sized bedroom with beige walls and the same white tile floor. A queen-sized bed with blue sheets stood against the far wall, atop a thick blue throw rug that expanded out most of the way over the room's floor. Better for bare feet that way. Two doors were on the rear wall, one ajar leading into the bathroom. The other was a closet, Bill presumed. A darkly-stained hardwood dresser standing against the wall opposite the bed completed the room's ensemble.

Not too bad.

Bill dropped the plastic bag containing the belongings that the prison had released back to him onto the bed and stepped into the bathroom. When he'd finished his business, he went back into the great room.

Joey was not alone. He stood in the entryway to the house not far from Bill's room, and he was flanked by a pair of utter hotties.

They both wore skin-tight black evening gowns that came to mid-thigh, diamonds in their ears, and gold necklaces on their throats. The one of the Joey's left was the taller of the two, and blonde, with flowing hair that fell well past her shoulders, smoldering green eyes, and the kind of tight body you'd expect from a dancer. To Joey's right was a brunette, with pixie cut hair. She was more curvy—Joey estimated a D cup—without being fat, and carried a trio of champagne flutes in one hand and an un-opened bottle of Dom in the other. They both smiled warmly at him when he emerged.

Joey was grinning ear to ear. "Bill. Meet Tami," he touched the blonde's shoulder, then the brunette's, "and Ricki."

It was all Bill could do to manage a surprised, "Hi."

The girls looked at each other, then Ricki stepped forward.

She walked slowly, seductively past him, heading toward the guest room. "Hi Bill," she said as she reached his shoulder, "we're your freedom party."

Bill swallowed, following her with his eyes. A light touch on his shoulder brought his attention around to Tami, who was tracing her fingertips down his arm until they reached his elbow. Then she slipped her arm into his and began gently turning him toward the guest room door. "Come on, handsome," she said in a smoky voice, and Bill's knees almost buckled.

It had been a long, long, long, long, *long* time. Really damn long.

He didn't even think about not going with them.

Just before he stepped back into the guest room, he looked back and saw Joey still standing there with that shit eating grin.

"Welcome back to the world, buddy," Joey said.

BILL FOUND Joey the next morning sitting at his kitchen counter, dressed in a blue bathrobe and drinking a cup of coffee. As he walked up, dressed in only his boxer briefs, Joey looked him over and raised an eyebrow, then shrugged.

"Coffee's in the machine," he said.

Bill walked around the counter and fished around in the cabinets for a bit until he found Joey's stash of coffee mugs, then he poured himself a cup.

It was good. Anything was, compared with the swill they served in the clink. But still, this was outstanding. He swirled the coffee in his mouth, savoring the flavor, then swallowed and raised an eyebrow Joey's way.

Joey chuckled. "Good shit, eh?"

Bill nodded. He leaned onto the counter, across from Joey,

and rested his elbows on the countertop. "Thanks for last night."

Joey grinned lasciviously. "I'd say it's my pleasure but it's more yours, right?" He glanced sidelong at the clock mounted the adjacent wall. It was almost 7:30. "Girls haven't taken off yet, have they?"

Bill shook his head.

"Good. I paid for the whole night until 9 this morning. And multiple shots on goal." Joey looked back at Bill and his grin twisted into a smirk. "If I were you I'd make sure to get another nut or two from each of them before they leave."

Bill nodded slowly. He'd take that under advisement. But enticing as that idea was, he had more pressing matters on his mind. "So. Rachel and Jason."

Joey's smirk faded into a businesslike expression. He looked down at the mug in his hands and sighed. "Yeah. Well, Jason split town right after High School. Bounced around a bit, but I hear he's up in Philly now." He looked back up, meeting Bill's eyes again, clearly reluctant to go any further.

"And Rachel?"

"You can't let it go, man? I know how you feel, but - "

Bill growled to cut Joey off, and found he was clenching his mug so hard his hand was shaking. He shoved his chin out, fixing Joey with his "Mess With Me And Die" prison yard stare. "You don't fucking know how I feel." He drew a deep breath, and releasing his mug, stabbed the air between himself and Joey with his index finger. "Fifteen years! That bitch stole fifteen years of my life. Fifteen years without my son - !"

Joey recoiled in alarm, and Bill realized he was shouting. He stopped.

Joey raised his hands, palms out toward Bill, and spoke slowly. "I mean I understand, ok?" He paused, then when Bill did not respond said again, "Ok?"

Bill took a breath to get control of himself, then nodded. "Yeah. Sorry."

"Look man, all I'm saying is you just got *out* of the clink. Why do you want to do something to get yourself thrown back in? You gone all institutional on me?"

Bill paused at the paralleling of his thoughts from the previous night. Was he just angling for a way to get back to the place that, terrible as it was, had become familiar, almost home?

He shook his head. "I can't let it go, brother."

Joey looked him in the eye for a long several seconds then, with a sigh, nodded. "Ok. Rachel's still in town, down in the 'hood. She's not doing so well, what I hear. I got her address from a guy I know. You can…well…" He left the rest unsaid.

Bill nodded his thanks. "You got my stuff?"

"Yeah." Joey pushed himself back from the counter and straightened. "One sec." He turned and left the kitchen, heading toward the hallway leading to his bedroom. A few minutes later, he came back with a black duffle bag that was stuffed to the gills. He set the bag down on the counter and slid it toward Bill. "Here you go."

Bill unzipped the bag and opened it. Here were all the rest of his worldly possessions. A couple pairs of pants, some shirts, and boxers. His copy of Crime And Punishment and his baseball card collection. His DD-214. A few other nicknacks and books. And there, at the bottom of the bag, a stainless steel revolver with a black grip and a box of .357 Magnum rounds. The serial numbers had been acid-etched away long before Bill went to the clink, and it had been his favorite gun for a long, long time.

He was ready for business.

"Thanks, man." He zipped up the duffle bag and downed the last of his coffee. Then he picked up the bag and headed back toward the guest room.

Joey had a point about the girls, after all.

<hr>

BILL COULD TELL it was Rachel weaving down the sidewalk from half a block away. It was something about the way she held herself, the way she moved. Even after all these years, and a whole lot of booze, drugs, or both tonight, that distinctive sway of her hips had not gone away.

He sat behind the wheel of Joey's car, across the street and a building over from her apartment complex. Although that was doing the dilapidated, gang-sign tagged heap of bricks where she lived more credit than it was due. The place looked like it should have been condemned before Bill went away, and hadn't been kept up since then.

And he thought the cell block had looked depressing.

It was late. Almost 1 in the morning, and most of the street traffic had died away. Only the occasional car came driving past, moving quickly down the lines of parallel-parked cars that flanked the street's two lanes so as to get through this neighborhood as quickly as possible. And the last group of pedestrians had swaggered past, hooping and hollering at each other in drunken revelry, about ten minutes ago.

It was just her, making her slow, meandering progress from the illumination of one street light to the next as she approached her building, and him.

She had on a black trench coat, though it had not been raining, and had her strawberry blond—probably going to grey now like Bill's was—hair pulled back in a ponytail that didn't quite touch the coat's collar. Looked like pumps on her feet, though he couldn't make out the color. Very nearly stripper heels.

Bill ran his hand beneath the leather jacket he was wearing and traced his fingertips along the grip of his revolver, tucked into his belt on his right hip, and could not keep an anticipatory smile from his lips.

He got out of the car and closed the door gently, so as to not make a lot of noise, then set off up the street in the direction she was coming from. His plan was to pass her, then loop around and follow her back to her building.

But he needn't have bothered. She never looked in his direction, and the way she kept staggering from one side of the sidewalk to the other he wondered if she really noticed anything at all.

Another car sped past in his direction, illuminating her face for a second before it continued on its way. Sure enough she had her eyes fixed firmly on the sidewalk in front of her. Oblivious.

Bill went ahead and crossed the street as soon as he was past her, and stopped behind a late-model mustang that had somehow not been keyed, tagged, or had its tires slashed. She was near to the entrance to her building now, and had stopped to fish around in her purse for something, probably her keys.

A few seconds later, she staggered forward again, all but falling into the door. It took a good thirty seconds for her to fumble with the keys before she found the right one and let herself in.

Bill was moving before she finished stepping through the door, hurrying to get there before the door swung shut; he didn't have the key and he hadn't tried to pick a lock in sixteen years.

He just made it, sticking his hand into the gap between the door and its frame with only a couple inches to go. He paused there and peeked in before opening it further.

Rachel had proceeded onward without a backward glance. He caught a glimpse of her turning right around a corner ahead before she passed out of sight.

He followed.

The interior of the building was as unappealing as the exterior. The carpet used to be burgundy but was holed in so many places, and stained in so many others, that it could not claim that honor any more. The yellowish paint on the walls was peeling, and there were noticeable cracks in the crown molding. Several of the cracks ran straight across the ceiling, and there were a bunch of water stains there as well.

Rachel sure was keeping herself in style.

Bill peeked around the corner, and saw her stopped in front of an apartment about halfway down the adjoining hall, on the left. Again she was fumbling with her keys; she dropped them this time before she was able to get them sorted out. A moment later she was inside, and he set out down the hall toward her door.

He expected he would have to knock, but when he reached her apartment, number seven, he found the door a couple inches ajar.

So much the easier.

He pushed the door open and stepped through. And stopped.

Rachel's apartment was in even worse condition than the building. There was a hole in the wall to the right of the door, where a coat hook might have been at some point. To the left, her tiny kitchen was covered in grime like it hadn't been cleaned in a month. Dirty pans were piled in the sink, and the counter was littered with empty bottles of cheap beer or liquor of all varieties. A bong, with the charred nub from the last joint to be smoked in it, stood prominently in a place of honor near the front.

The living room, directly ahead, had a sagging old beige sofa directly across from the door and beneath a single long window that spanned the length of the room. The curtains, once white but now grey from dirt and years of smoke, were closed, blocking the view of a brick wall unless Bill missed his guess. In front of the sofa stood a coffee table that might had been stained red-brown at one point but was now so scratched and covered in cigarette burns it didn't matter. An old-school TV—as in, the kind that was in existence before Bill went away —sat against the wall to the left, a yellow folding chair sitting directly in front of it.

The entire place smelled of cigarette and marijuana smoke, despite the pathetic attempts of a plug-in air freshener in a wall outlet beneath the hole in the wall.

Rachel stood with her back to the door in front of the coffee table, messing with her earrings.

Bill just looked at her for a long couple of seconds.

She was thin. Much thinner than the lushly-curved woman who had used to be his wife. Her hair was greying, but it had thinned also. Age had caught up to her as well, it seemed. Well, it wouldn't do any more catching after tonight.

Bill drew the revolver and let it hang in his hand by his right thigh, then he kicked the door shut with his heel. It made a loud THUNK as it shut, and Rachel jumped.

She spun around, her eyes widening in alarm. "What the fuck do you think you're - "

Bill interrupted her. "Hello, Rachel."

She narrowed her eyes, but no recognition appeared on her face. He took a step toward her and smiled thinly. "Don't recognize me?"

He knew he had changed during his time in the clink. His hairline had receded, and he had developed frown lines around his mouth and eyes. He'd also lost a lot of body fat; all that great prison food. But he was still the man he had been when they were together all those years ago.

Of course, had he not known who she was he might not have placed her as his former wife, turned betrayer.

She looked like hell. Her face had always been narrow; now it was gaunt, to match the excessive skinniness of the rest of her frame. Her eyes were sunken pits, with dark shadows beneath them that looked permanent. Her skin was pock-marked, and her hair was thin, brittle-looking. She wasn't wrinkled like he was so much as withered, and there was a wildness about her that belied that complete lack of life or soul in her eyes.

Part of him cringed to look at her.

It took a few seconds for it to register with her, then she nodded. "So you got out, huh? Good for you. Not sure what - "

"Where's the money, Rachel?"

He moved another step closer. She half-snorted, half spat and spread her hands out, but she didn't reply.

"You and Ronnie stole half a million dollars, and pinned it on me." Another step.

She shook her head and let out a bitter almost-laugh. "There is no money, Bill. Ronnie took it and ran off six months after you went in. This," she swept her hand around the pit of an apartment, "is all I got." She made a drunkenly exaggerated "go away" wave with her left hand in his general direction.

And Ronnie was in the clink now, or so Bill had been told, and wouldn't be getting out while he was still vertical. Bill had expected Ronnie would screw her over, but he still couldn't wrap his head around how Rachel could have been so stupid as to trust a guy like him.

Then again, it really was more like she had come to hate Bill, and wanted to get back at him over that girl in Kansas City. And she hadn't cared about how, or with whom.

He sighed and looked down at the floor before his feet. He'd long since come to terms with the part he had played in his own demise. If he hadn't cheated…

It didn't excuse what she did. Nothing could.

Still…

"You ever hear from our son?" He looked back up at her

face in time to see her grimace, as though the very idea was distasteful to her.

"Nah, he's out in Vegas or something." Vegas. Of course she wouldn't know where Jason was. "Don't want nothing to do with - " Her words cut off as she finally looked at him fully. And saw the gun.

She swallowed, hard. "You here to kill me, that it?" She sounded decidedly neutral about the entire concept.

Bill did not answer.

A second passed, and a change came over her. She adjusted her balance so that her right hip stuck out in that pose she used to use that was so damn sexy, and a slow smile appeared on her face. Problem was, on her overly thin frame the pose seemed stilted, and the smile that was supposed to be seductive was sick, twisted.

"Or maybe you want to get it on, for old time's sake?" She tugged at the belt on her trench coat. The knot that had been holding the coat loosened, and the coat slid off her shoulders onto the floor.

She was nude beneath it.

Bill had cringed before upon seeing her face. The rest of her... She must have been coming back from a trick, but who would pay for *that*?

The woman he had known and loved, the lushly curved and sensuous soul who had so completely turned him on before, was gone.

The breasts that she used to love smothering him with were no more. They flopped down her torso like water balloons that had been drained of fluid leaving only the rubber behind, and part of her left nipple was gone, like it had been ripped away. Or bitten off. The bones of her hips stuck out through her skin, and her ribs showed through. Her skin seemed to hang off her, and stretch marks that their son had not caused before Bill went away rippled across her belly. The pockmarks that blemished her face continued everywhere else on her body, and scabs further desecrated her skin. Her pubic hair was as thin and ratty as that atop her head, and he thought he saw a scab or two there also.

Track marks were clearly visible on her arms…and was that another one on her inner thigh?

He found himself retreating, and she advanced on him in a slow, hip-rolling gait that was probably supposed to be sexy but just came off as an obscene perversion of beauty.

"How about it, Bill?" She had closed the distance between them without him realizing it. She traced a finger down his chest to his belly before alighting on the top of his belt. This close, the smell of her sweat overwhelmed the faint strawberry perfume she was wearing.

She licked her cracked lips, and the sight made him raise the gun instinctively.

Rachel met the gun with her left hand, and drew her fingers sensually down its length.

"Come on, baby," she sank down to her knees in front of him, and guided the gun forward so it filled the space between them. "You remember how good it was."

She bent forward and kissed the gun's muzzle. She turned her head to his right and moved down the barrel towards his hand, kissing the cold metal the entire way. Then her tongue flicked out, and she ran it back up the barrel, then across the muzzle and down the other side.

Bill squirmed as memories flooded into him, how she used to do that to him, and how good she made it.

She looked up and met his eyes with hers as her tongue finished running down the left side of the barrel, and she gave his thumb a light kiss.

Cold, dead eyes that showed no joy, no sensuality, no feeling of any kind. Eyes without a soul behind them.

Whatever arousal Bill had been feeling from the memories

of their previous time together fled beneath the reality of the…thing…kneeling before him. At least the hookers Joey had bought for him were good actresses: they had made it seem as though they really enjoyed what they were doing with him, that it had brought them some pleasure above and beyond the money they had received.

In fairness, they had actually seemed to really enjoy being *together*, but that was not relevant just then.

There was not even a facsimile of desire or pleasure in the gaze of the creature before him—Bill could not bear to give it the name that his former love used, once upon a time. Only emptiness and resignation over an act to be performed, and beneath it an all-consuming and insatiable need, looked up at him.

Reflexively, he cocked the hammer of the revolver back.

Rachel froze, her eyes locked on his. "No?" She let out a breath and her shoulders sagged, then she nodded, ever so slightly. "Fine." She placed both hands around the barrel—the same way she used to grip him, back in the day—but instead of guiding it to her mouth, she moved the muzzle dead center on her forehead.

"Do it."

She stared up at him, and he met her gaze. A tear formed in the corner of her right eye and flowed down her cheek.

"Go on." Her voice was becoming more insistent.

His index finger moved inside the trigger guard and rested on the trigger. Then he paused, just looking at her.

"DO IT!" She was shouting now, but it wasn't anger or fear behind that shout.

He saw it in her dead, soulless eyes.

She was living in her own private little hell, her every day a misery of despair and hopelessness. Every man preyed upon her, every woman competed against or belittled her. There was no solace, no rest, except for the needle…and that would not do for long.

Rachel's daily existence was a punishment far greater than any he could ever dream to dole out. The bullet would be a release, a mercy. And from the faint glimmer of hope in her eyes he saw she knew it, just as she knew she would never have the courage to do it herself.

No.

Bill lowered the hammer and stepped back, pulling the revolver out of her hands.

Rachel lost her balance and fell, face-first, to the floor, only catching herself on her elbows at the last second. She looked up at him, and that glimmer of hope faded, leaving only empty despair.

"Goodbye, Rachel." Bill turned away from her and tucked the revolver back into his belt, then moved toward the door.

She was silent until he had the door open, then -

"You dickless bastard! Get back here! You spineless little pussy! You - "

He let the invectives, the insults, the obscenity wash over him as he left her apartment. He knew it was not him she was screaming at.

Halfway down the hall, her shouts turned into an incoherent scream of primal fury.

By the time he reached the outer door, fury had given way to soul-destroying despair, and her scream had turned into a series of sobbing wails.

Six months of working the sorry-ass job his PO got for him. Six months of crashing in Joey's spare room and keeping his nose meticulously clean. Six months of not going out, and saving every penny he got. And finally, Bill obtained permission to leave the state.

He bought a jalopy and drove the five hours up the Delmarva peninsula to Philly, to one particular neighborhood.

The Web had existed before he went away, but everything was easier now, more connected. It hadn't been hard to find out where to go.

He sat in his car, looking at the apartment complex where Jason lived, and realized he was afraid. More afraid than he had been on his first day in the clink. More afraid than when he had asked Rachel, heart in his hand, to marry him. More afraid than when he'd made his first jump in Airborne training.

It had been so long. The boy he knew was gone. Jason was a man of twenty-two now, and probably full of anger with the father who had left him behind, so many years ago, to go to prison.

This was stupid. He wouldn't want to see Bill, let alone talk with him. Better to just head back to Hampton now, save himself the heartache and embarrassment.

Instead of starting the car and driving away, Bill opened the door and got out. He squared his shoulders and marched across the street through a gap in the traffic, and into the apartment complex.

The complex was one of those horseshoe-shaped arrangements, with an opening to the outside world at one end, a playground and swimming pool in the center, and two levels of apartments in the ring around the pool. The courtyard was planted with bushes and flowers around the pool, and a couple of elms back by the playground, giving the entire place a homey, relaxing feel. The swimming pool was empty, but a couple of moms sat on a bench by the playground and watched as a half dozen kids screamed and ran around on the playground.

Nice place.

The manager's office was on Bill's left as he walked into the courtyard, but he paid it no mind. He knew where he was going.

A set of black painted, wrought-iron stairs to his right led up to the second level. He ascended the stairs, paying little heed to the ominous creak they gave as he placed his weight onto the second-to-last step. Then he was on the second level, and he looked around.

The door closest to him read 232 on a brass label plate beneath the dirt-brown door's peephole.

Bill pulled a folded up sheet of paper out of his pocket and checked it. Jason was apartment 217. Probably about halfway around.

He set out, and sure enough almost exactly on the opposite side of the ring from that first place, he stopped in front of the door labelled 217.

There was a mat set out in front of the door, the cheery "Welcome" ringed by creeping green vines from which bloomed purple and pink flowers.

Bill stepped onto the mat and faced the door, and the peephole seemed to stare at him. Through him.

Doubt, fear, and excitement battled in his chest, but doubt most of all. Did he really think Jason wanted to see him? And even if he did, did Bill really have the right to impose on him now, before he really had himself together?

Again the impulse to turn around and head back to Hampton reared up inside him.

Instead, Bill drew a deep breath, squared his shoulders, and knocked on the door.

The Suspect's Wife

A Davidson & Harper Mystery

Michael Kingswood

The Suspect's Wife

A client's cryptic story leads Private Investigators Ronald Harper and Kathleen Davidson to evidence of multiple murders.

R onald Harper shut the door of his car, a late model Outback that was painted a shade of blue so dark most people thought it was black, and thumbed the remote on his keychain. The squawk of the doors locking elicited a slight smile, as it always did. It was good to get around in style.

The early autumn morning was cool, but not uncomfortable, as he walked the hundred yards from the parking lot to his office building. It was almost not worth wearing his leather jacket, but the weather guessers had predicted a cold front was going to roll in later in the day, maybe bringing rain with It. And besides, he had an image to maintain.

The simple swinging door pulled open easily. Kathleen must already be inside; she was the only other person who had a key. Hardly a surprise. She was far more a morning person than he. With a wry grin, Ronald let the door swing shut behind him and took the narrow staircase beyond two at a time. As always, by the time he reached the top, he felt more energetic. Nothing like getting the blood pumping to wake a fellow up.

The staircase ended at a wood door that contained a translucent window in its upper half. The words, "Davidson and Harper, Private Investigators" were stenciled into the window in black tape.

Home sweet home.

He pushed the door open and walked into the familiar office. He instantly felt his mood improve. There was something about the dark-stained wood panelling on the walls, the weathered leather couch off to one side, his and Kathleen's desks against the back wall, the narrow window between them that looked out onto the river, the smell of leather, paper, cigarettes, and secrets that made him feel comfortable.

He grinned at Kathleen as he entered and received her usual half-smirk in response.

"Ron. Out late with Isabel again?"

He shrugged. "Not too late. She had an early meeting today." He stepped around the coffee table in front of the couch and circled around to his desk chair. It was pricey. Ergonomically precise, or so the salesman said. Whatever. It was the most comfy office chair Ronald had ever sat in, and was worth every penny. "Anything brewing?"

Kathleen shook her head. "Just the coffee." She raised her mug to her lips and took a drink before adding, "Which is running low, by the way. It's your turn to buy."

Ronald nodded. He didn't need her to remind him of that. But then, she was the one for details. It showed from the way she dressed. Always an impeccable business suit. Whether with pants or a skirt, she always looked her best. This morning, she wore dark blue; he noted she seemed to wear blue more often than not. Probably because it set off her eyes well. She was not his type; he generally did not prefer blondes. And even if he had, she was his partner, not a potential hookup. But all the same, he had to admit she always managed to look good.

Ronald chuckled inwardly as he wondered how many of their clients signed on because of how she looked even more than their firm's reputation as a top-notch investigating unit. She would probably rip his heart out if he suggested it, but he could think of at least two in the last month who had only come around after meeting them….her…in person. A lesser man would feel slighted for that, but whatever brought in the cash sat well with Ronald.

"We've got a ten o'clock."

Ronald glanced at the clock. Nine fifty.

"What's the deal?"

Kathleen shrugged. "Some kind of family trouble, from the sound of it."

Great. Another job chasing after some bimbo's husband, trying to get pictures of him in the act with the "other woman". Sometimes it turned out they really were fooling around, but Ronald was almost always appalled by the women those guys chose as mistresses. If you're going to risk your marriage and screw up your financial future, at least go for someone hot! But no, a lot of the time those guys hooked up with fat trolls. No accounting for some men's thought processes, he supposed.

"Well at least it's a pay check." Ronald tried to put more cheeriness into his voice than he thought.

Kathleen snorted.

Fifteen minutes passed quickly. A cup of coffee and the morning paper saw to that. But by a few minutes after ten, Ronald began to get annoyed. Maybe it was the Marine Corps refusing to let him go, but people who were not punctual were very…

A firm knock on the door broke Ronald's chain of thought. He looked up and saw a man silhouetted beyond the translucent glass. He exchanged glances with Kathleen, then stood and pulled the door open.

And was just about bowled over as the man shoved his way into the room. He was not overly tall, about Ronald's height, but he was broad, with the shoulders of a linebacker and the musculature to match. His face was round and dominated by a hooked nose that almost made one not notice the thin, almost feminine lips around his mouth. He had black hair that hung limply to his eyebrows in front and was cut short in back. He dressed simply, in jeans - Levi's Ronald noted - and a plain white t-shirt beneath a maroon windbreaker.

As the man swept past, Ronald recovered his balance and pushed the door closed. He flipped the deadbolt and pulled the roll-up curtain that hung at the top of the door's window down, then turned back toward the man. Or rather, his back.

The man had eyes only for Kathleen. "Ms. Davidson?" he asked. His voice was a high baritone, almost a tenor, which did not fit with his hulking form very well at all. He sounded nervous.

Kathleen smiled winningly at him and rose from her desk chair. "Good morning, Mr. Samuelson." She extended her hand and he shook it quickly, as though as an afterthought. "This is my partner, Ronald Harper."

The man, Samuelson, blinked and looked aside toward Ronald as though seeing him for the first time. And no wonder, the way he had barged in. He swallowed and managed an apologetic smile. "Nice to meet you." He did not offer his hand to shake.

"Likewise," Ronald said. He returned to his desk and leaned back against its front edge, folding his hands over his chest. This client was not very impressive so far. "What can we do for you, Mr. Samuelson?"

Samuelson opened his mouth, then paused. He looked away from Ronald, toward the door and for a moment Ronald thought he was going to flee. Then he swallowed and spoke, his eyes still directed elsewhere.

"I think someone killed my wife."

RONALD GAZED through his binoculars at a little house on a hill. It was the only building for miles. No surprise there. It had taken forty-five minutes on the Interstate to get there from town. As always, he was amazed how quickly civilization faded once one got outside the city limits and past the suburbs.

The house was simple: square-shaped, painted white with a shingle roof. It had a small porch out front and a meandering driveway that disappeared in the trees as it descended the hill. Its address placed it on the road Ronald was parked on the side of, which meant either the road curved mightily as it approached the hill or the driveway was excessively long. He was betting on the later.

"That surely doesn't look like the scene of a grizzly crime," he mused. That much was certain. Ronald was quite sure when he and Kathleen got up there they would find nothing more interesting than an old lady with her cats, or at best a country couple who preferred to be alone now that the kids had flown the coop. Certainly not a cold-blooded killer. "Ten to one she just ran off with some guy and Samuelson's making things up in his own mind."

On the seat next to him, Kathleen smirked but said nothing.

"And why the hell didn't he go to the cops if he thought…" Ronald stopped talking. He did not need to finish that thought to know the answer. Sometimes you needed justice, not law. And so you don't go to the cops. But in those times, people generally take matters into their own hands, not hire PIs.

He rolled his eyes. The hell with it. It was a paycheck. Not that he was going to kill anyone; if it was what Samuelson thought, Ronald intended to call the cops himself quick as can be. It was Samuelson's problem if he needed to spend a bunch of money so that someone else could make the call, not him.

"You set?"

Kathleen nodded. "Just waiting on you."

Ronald chuckled and put the Outback in gear.

The driveway was every bit as long, and quite a bit more steep, as it appeared from down below, but eventually they pulled out from underneath the gold and red of leaves that were getting ready to fall and emerged in the small yard in front of the house.

Up close, the house was quite a bit less appealing that it had been from afar. The paint was peeling in many places. One of the shutters on the front windows was knocked askew. And the roof was in dire need of re-shingling. Weeds grew tall in the remains of a flower bed below the front porch, and it looked as though the owners had not mowed the lawn in a week.

"Nice place," Kathleen said, her tone more than a little ironic, as they exited the car.

Ronald was forced to agree.

He took a moment to verify his Glock was sitting properly in its holster in the small of his back, then he set off toward the house. Kathleen followed at his right. She, like Ronald, was constantly scanning the area, her expression wary but not nervous. He noticed, though, that her left hand never strayed far from her hip, where she wore her piece on a holster at her waist, beneath her light jacket.

The steps leading to the front porch creaked slightly as Ronald stepped up, and for a moment he pictured himself breaking through and falling hip-deep through a hole just large enough for one leg. The thought of such a ridiculous predicament lent extra speed to his stride, and the step did not give way anyway. All the same, when he reached the top it was with just a tiny bit of relief.

Kathleen looked at him askance. "You alright?"

He spread his hands and grinned for a second, nodding.

Her sniff spoke volumes.

The front door was, once upon a time, painted red and inlaid with a brass knocker. But, like everywhere else on the house, the paint was peeling, revealing the underlying wood. And it looked as though no one had polished the brass in decades, it had so much verdigris. Narrow windows stood on either side of the door, running its entire length, but the view inside was obscured by drab-looking hanging drapes.

The only sound was the noise of his and Kathleen's breathing, and the rustle of the breeze through the tree limbs back at the clearing's edge.

"Something's not right here," Ronald said. "Didn't

Samuelson say someone lives here? I'd say we're the first people to set foot on this porch in a year."

Kathleen did not reply at first, instead moving to the right, toward another window, longer like the kind people mount in their living rooms. Ronald could see from where he was the glass was cracked in several places. She looked through it for a short moment, then glanced back at him.

"I don't see any movement." The same doubt he felt had crept into her voice. What sort of half-assed wild goose chase had Samuelson set them on?

Ronald and Kathleen traded looks. He was half-inclined to just say "Screw it" and go home, but he could tell from Kathleen's expression she would have none of that. And she had a point; Samuelson had paid them a retainer, after all. But still…

"Alright, let's get it done," he said with resignation.

Ronald stepped up to the door, his right hand slipping behind his back to grasp the grip of his Glock. To his side, Kathleen also made ready to draw. He glanced back at her, and she nodded.

Ronald knocked, a quick powerful staccato that should have been clearly audible throughout the house.

After what seemed like forever, but in fact was only a minute when Ronald checked his watch, there was neither an answer at the door nor any sound from within.

He knocked again. Still nothing. It looked like they had to do it the hard way. He hated the hard way.

Ronald stepped back and made a sweeping gesture from Kathleen toward the door. "You're up," he said. She was the locksmith of their pair, not he.

Kathleen rolled her eyes, but got down to business without commenting. Her expression said enough.

She retrieved a set of tools from the inner pocket of her jacket and crouched down before the doorknob. As Ronald kept watch, both on the interior of the house and the yard and tree line, she fiddled around with a pair of long, needle-like implements. After a few brief moments poking and prodding, there was an audible CLICK.

Nodding in satisfaction, Kathleen replaced the tools and straightened. She rolled her shoulders slowly then drew her Sig Sauer. Ronald did not say how awkward the large weapon looked in her small hands. She would kick his ass for that, and besides he knew well that she was a crack shot with it. Instead, he drew his Glock and assumed a ready stance.

Kathleen glanced back at him and he nodded. At his signal, she pulled the door open and he charged through.

The inside of the house was dim, dusty, and filled with unpleasant smells: mildew, but beneath that a rank odor that he could not place though it nagged at him. The door opened into the living room, which was sparsely filled with a couple chairs and a small couch, all of which were covered in cloth, as though the owner had closed up the house for the season. That had to have been a number of seasons ago, though, as a thick layer of dust covered everything.

"Classy place," Ronald muttered.

He stalked over to the sole exit from the room: a doorway that was filled with hanging beads that had long since lost their luster. The hallway beyond led left to a pair of bedrooms and a bathroom, and right to a kitchen. All were as sparsely furnished and dust-filled as the living room. Except for the kitchen.

"Well look at what we have here," Kathleen said as the pair surveyed the scene.

The kitchen was L-shaped, with counters containing a sink and an electric stove along the rear wall of the house. On the wall opposite stood a refrigerator alongside extensive cabinets and shelving. At the bend of the L lay a breakfast nook complete with a table and chairs which stood before a bay window that overlooked the downslope of the hillside and the valley below. A windowed door to the left of the table led to the back yard. To the table's right, at the end of the L, was a moderate sized alcove where a pot rack hung next to a baker's rack, which stood next to a closed door. The room was painted a cheerful yellow, with paintings of flowering vines curling around every corner and along the edge of the ceiling. The floor was ceramic tile and the countertops granite. Overall, a well put-together kitchen.

And it was immaculate. Not a trace of dust dirtied the room, in stark contrast with the rest of the house. Clearly someone had been here. Often. Why would they only frequent the kitchen, and not the rest of the house?

"Looks like they've been using the back door," Kathleen said, crouching down near that door and examining the lock. "It's not been jimmied."

"Hmm. I wonder where…" Ronald turned the knob on the door near the baker's rack and pulled it open. The door creaked softly; the hinges required some WD-40. Beyond, a set of rickety stairs descended into darkness The cellar.

Ronald looked back at Kathleen, who pursed her lips for a moment in thought. Finally she shrugged. "Might as well."

They went down slowly, Ronald leading the way. A lone lightbulb dangled from the ceiling, providing dim illumination to the stairs, but after about a dozen steps, they turned left and that small illumination was mostly lost.

Ronald slowed, flexing his fingers on the grip of his Glock as his eyes adjusted to the suddenly increased gloom. Ahead, he could vaguely make out the outline of an empty doorframe. Beyond was only shadow. This was not going to do at all. He stopped and reached into the inner pocket of his leather jacket where he always carried a penlight. There was certainly another light around somewhere, but damned if he wanted to fumble around in the darkness until he found it.

The beam of his penlight caught details here and there. A

desk against the wall with a bulletin board hanging above it. A chest of some sort in the corner. A bed - a cot? - In the other corner. Another door?

And then the lights came on, making Ronald blink at the sudden glare. Acting on instinct, he leapt to the right and dropped into a crouch, Glock rising to firing position as he spun around.

And saw Kathleen standing just inside the doorway, he fingers on the light switch right next to the doorway and a bemused expression on her face.

"Christ!" Ronald muttered as he lowered the Glock and stood up straight.

Kathleen shook her head and chuckled. "Why so jumpy, Ron? I mean really..." Her words drifted off and her eyes widened.

Ron turned, following her gaze to the bulletin board. What he saw there sent a chill running down his spine.

* * *

GREGORY BARNES WAS every bit the cliché homicide detective. From the cheap suit to the bad tie to the constant scowl and the "I think I'm a tough guy" attitude. Ronald hated him on sight. Problem was, he was stuck with him.

Had they discovered the items in the cellar back in town, Ronald had a number of contacts in the Department he could call to grease the skids, or at least edit the official report so that he and Kathleen would not be mentioned in it, or bothered by it. Out here in the boonies, though...

"You want to tell me why in the hell you didn't call us as soon as you got done talking with your client?" Jesus, Barnes even *sounded* like a guy from a bad cop show.

Ronald sat in one of the interrogation rooms at the County Sheriff's department. It was pretty much the same as every other interrogation room he had ever seen. Small but not cramped, dominated by a single table with four chairs. No windows, but a great big mirror; it didn't take much imagination to figure out what was on the other side or that. A single door leading to the rest of the precinct. Office. Whatever they called it out here.

It had taken the cops about twenty minutes to arrive at the house. And less than five to throw cuffs on he and Kathleen and haul them down to the station for questioning. Ronald was not a cop, sure. Never had been. But he and Kathleen did work in law enforcement…sort of. Most of the time there was a certain amount of professional consideration given between them and the cops. At least in town. Apparently not here though.

It was more than a little annoying.

"I'd rather not, no. Thanks for asking." It was probably a mistake to be a wise-ass to a guy like Barnes. Ah what the hell, he was a douchebag and Ronald was getting sick to death of the rigamarole.

Barnes' scowl grew more pronounced, and for a moment Ronald almost thought he was going to take a swing at him. Fortunately, Barnes was not a *complete* amateur. Instead of striking Ronald, he brought his hand down on the table between them with a loud SMACK. "Goddamnit, this is not a fucking game, Harper. I've got you on Breaking and Entering, Interfering with a Police Investigation…'

Ronald snorted. B&E was penny-ante shit, and they both knew it. And the other… "Hey, we called you, didn't we? As soon as we found those pictures."

"*After* you already tainted the scene. We'll be lucky to get anything useful with all the prints you two left down there." Barnes' eyes narrowed and he leaned forward in a manner that Ronald imagined was supposed to be intimidating. It just made him look stupid. "But maybe that's the point. Maybe your so-called client is your alibi, and you called us in order to deflect attention from yourselves."

He could *not* be serious. Could he?

But looking in Barnes' eyes, Ronald could see the detective meant every word he said. Inane as it sounded, he really believed he was on to something, or at least he thought he was being clever and was going to wheedle additional information out of Ronald that way.

It was too much. Ronald could not stop himself. He began to chuckle, then as Barnes' face began to flush with what Ronald could only assume was anger - it should have been embarrassment, as stupid as he was being - his chuckle became a full-on guffaw that lasted for a long couple of minutes.

The whole while, Barnes sat in silence, growing more and more red as his jaw worked. The little artery on his temple throbbed so hard the Ronald halfway expected it to burst.

"Finished?" Barnes demanded as Ronald got his laughter under control.

"I am." Ronald pushed his chair back and stood. "It's been a fun chat, but I have work to do." He began walking around the table toward the exit.

"Siddown," Barnes said. Hell, practically shouted.

Ronald stopped walking, but did not sit, instead favoring Barnes with a look that he hoped conveyed the full extent of his exasperation. "We're wasting time, Detective. I've told you everything I know. I'm sure Kathleen has done the same with your partner. Instead of continuing to beat this dead horse, we really should…"

Barnes rose suddenly, moving far more quickly and gracefully than Ronald would have given him credit for. Maybe there was more to the guy than he thought. He had Ronald by several inches, and managed to affect a somewhat effective loom. "*We* are not doing anything. You and your partner, assuming the County Attorney does not decide to press charges, are going back home and you're not going to put a foot anywhere *near* this case. We've got the ball here, and we sure don't need the likes of you meddling and hanging around underfoot." He drew in a deep breath, the air making a faint rasping sound as it entered his nostrils. "You got that, Harper?"

Ronald almost burst out laughing again, but thought the better of it. Clearly Barnes was the kind of guy who liked to think events proceeded solely the way he directed. Better to just let him have his delusions. Ronald nodded. "Got it, Detective."

Barnes looked into Ronald's eyes for a long moment. Then he gave a quick nod and gestured with his thumb toward the door. "Get the hell out of here."

RONALD SETTLED down into his desk chair and sighed contentedly. He had shopped a long time to find just the right unit for his office desk: padded without being excessively squishy, supportive without being board-like, on a swivel because…well just because, with arms long enough to comfortably rest his flesh and blood arms on and a headrest that extended above his shoulder blades. Kathleen had heckled him for a long time about how much it cost, but it was an investment worth making. That chair alone turned the days in the office into journeys to the lap of luxury. Mostly. Even better, he had caught Kathleen glancing enviously at it ever so often. She, of course, denied it.

So, despite the confusing nature of the case and the day's setback, Ronald felt quite content as he leaned back and lifted his drink—The McAllan 18, singe-malt, neat—to his lips.

"Where are we then?"

Kathleen frowned over at him from her desk - her chair was like a rock compared with his - and halfway lifted the notepad she was scanning so he could see it. "It doesn't add up," she replied. "Samuelson suspected foul play, but he didn't go to the cops."

"Because he wanted to leave his options open for payback."

She sounded doubtful. "He looked more scared than vengeful to me." She tapped at her lip with the pen in her hand for a moment, her eyes losing focus as she drifted off into thought.

Ronald had to concede that. Only having that one meeting to go by, Samuelson did not seem the type to act hastily, or emotionally. But then again, who knows what losing a spouse will drive a man to do. If someone did something to Isabel…

Ronald gave a little jerk, almost falling out of his chair in surprise. He and Isabel had only been seeing each other for a few months, since he helped her resolve an issue with her former fiancé involving his grandmother's wedding ring. He cared about her, sure. And not just because her father was filthy rich. Hell, he had almost had to cap a couple gumbah's to protect her during that wedding ring case. But he had not really thought very deeply about how he really felt for her. The sudden possessiveness and protectiveness he just found himself experiencing was…unexpected.

Ah hell. This was not the time to lose it over some girl. There were things to do.

But then, Isabel was not just some girl, was she?

"Ah to hell with it," Ronald said, gulping down the last of his scotch - actually most of his scotch; he had not been drinking it for very long - in a single swallow. "Let's call Samuelson and get some answers out of his chubby ass."

Kathleen peered at him in silence for a moment. "The cops are probably all over him, you know."

Ronald nodded.

"We promised the Sheriff's Department we would not get any further involved in the case."

Now it was Ronald's time to give Kathleen a level, mockingly incredulous stare. She could not be serious.

Finally, after about ten seconds, she snorted out a half-laugh and grinned. "Yeah, who am I kidding, right?" She pulled open her desk drawer and pulled out the firm's address book, a thick leather-bound tome that contained contact information on all their clients, starting way back before Kathleen tempted Ronald into partnering up with her.

Very quickly, Kathleen had the book open to the "S" section. She traced down the names until she found Samuelson's, then picked up the phone from its cradle on her desk and punched in the numbers.

Fifteen seconds later, she slammed the phone down and pushed herself back from her desk forcefully enough that the rollers on her chair's legs moved her all the way back into the wall.

"Kathleen, what - ?"

"It's disconnected."

The words hit him like a ton of bricks. "*What?*"

"Samuelson's phone is disconnected."

Oh shit. "You don't think - "

She cut him off, nodding in the affirmative with a grim expression on her face. "We're being set up."

"SON OF A BITCH." Ronald could not believe it. But eyes do not deceive. Most of the time. Alright, some of the time.

He sat in the passenger seat of Kathleen's car, a well-maintained Chevy Malibu that sported some special modifications a mechanic friend of hers was only too happy to install. She sat behind the wheel and, like him, stared through the windshield at a large brick building that was probably once a warehouse, but now was boarded up with yellow NO ENTRY tape strung in every doorway and window. That had not stopped people from breaking the window glass, with thrown rocks Ronald suspected. At the corner nearest them was a large sign advertising the construction project, due to start in less than a month, that would convert the old building into modern high-rent condos. Or condos anyway. Ronald was not willing to give odds what sort of rent the owners could get for them in this neighborhood.

All that was not particularly unusual or disturbing. What was disturbing was the street address of the condemned building matched the address Samuelson had given them as his place of residence.

"Son of a bitch." It bore repeating. "You sure this is the right address?"

Kathleen held up the note page where she had copied the information from the address book. 7657 Taylor Avenue. Yep, that was it. Son of a bitch.

"I don't suppose he was thinking about where he was *going* to live. You know, after the condos get built." Kathleen glowered at him and he raised his hands defensively. "Hey, just spitballing here. Son of a bitch."

"You've said that three times now, Ron."

"It's appropriate. So," he scowled deeply, "we've been had. But by whom, really? And why?" It was baffling. Ronald could not recall ever seeing Samuelson, or whoever he was, before in his life, and he had a good memory for faces and places.

"At least the cash he gave us is real."

There *was* that, at least. There are ways to test a bill to verify it is real and not counterfeit. It pained Ronald to go through the testing process, since it tended to destroy the test bills and they really needed the money; it had been a slow month at the office. But the bills passed with flying colors.

So why hire a couple of PIs for a bogus case, but pay them real money and send them to the hideout of a *real* serial killer?

The pictures on the wall in the cellar, depicting body parts that had been roughly hacked off and the badly beaten faces of a number of women, sure made it seem like a killer's hideout, anyway.

"He must be trying to cover his tracks."

Ronald blinked, Kathleen's words drawing him out of his musings and back to the present. "Huh?"

Kathleen rolled her eyes slightly. "Think about it. He's accomplished what he wanted to here, and he wants to make a getaway. But the evidence is out there, and he knows it could point to him. So he cooks up a story and gets a couple of patsies to wander in to muss up the evidence. Maybe they mess it up enough to make it unusable. Maybe they do *such* a good job the cops think *they* are the killers. At the least, it delays the investigation enough for him to slip away to the next town."

Ronald shook his head. "Too many holes; the cops would quickly realize the patsies were just that. And besides, you wouldn't hire PIs for that. You'd get people who don't know what the hell they're doing."

Kathleen opened her mouth, to object Ronald was certain, but after a moment shut it again, nodding in agreement. Reluctant agreement. "In that case I've got nothing." She sighed and twisted her hands on the grip of the steering wheel. "So what now?"

"Now?" Ronald looked back at the shell of a building before them. "Now we see if we can figure out who Samuelson really is. And how he's connected to the victims in the pictures."

"That's not going to be easy. We don't even know where to start looking for him, and we don't have the pictures…"

Ronald grinned at her and pulled his cell phone, complete with its built-in high definition camera, out of his pocket. He wagged the phone back and forth and Kathleen's lips turned upward into a grin.

JOHNNY TENNEBAUM WAS in his late thirties, balding, and sported a substantial beer belly that pulled his uniform shirt tight, tight enough that Ronald always wondered why the buttons had not popped off yet. How he managed to stay on the force, as big as he was, still surprised Ronald. But he had held the position as chief evidence clerk for the local precinct for three years, and he ran a tight ship: efficient, with a perfect accountability history and not even a hint of corruption. That sort of performance from someone in such a key position probably warranted some flexibility in other requirements, Ronald supposed.

"Ron! How's it going, devil dog," Johnny said in greeting as Ronald entered his office, Kathleen in tow. The cop's broad grin seemed to take up his entire face. It was the kind of cheery grin that would instantly put a person at ease, make you feel welcome. Word was he had coaxed many a confession out of perps with that grin, before he shifted over to the evidentiary logistics side of the world.

He never had explained, to Ronald's satisfaction, why he made that shift.

"Hey Johnny," Ron said, clasping hands with his friend. "You remember Kathleen?"

"Impossible to forget." Johnny winked at her impishly, but he was harmless enough. There was no way in hell he would ever cheat on Helen. He did not want to lose his kids and most of his pension. And, Ronald was quite sure she could easily kick his ass up the street and back down again, former Marine or no.

Kathleen nodded companionably to Johnny but did not return the wink. "Do you have a moment, Lieutenant Tennebaum?" She was sometimes no fun at all.

Johnny's grin faded, his expression becoming more shrewd. "So, not a social call, huh."

"Sorry, Johnny," Ronald said, and meant it. He hated having to call in favors from friends. Or at least, he hated calling in favors that could get friends in trouble. But he saw little choice.

Johnny nodded and, turning away, gestured for them to follow him. He led Ronald and Kathleen past the caged-in desk where Johnny's duty clerks sat and maintained watch of the evidence vaults, then around the corner and into his private office. It was nothing fancy, just a simple desk in a corner and a half-dozen file cabinets against the opposite wall, but in his time on the job Johnny had made it somewhat homey. Pictures of his family sat on the desk, plaques and award citations hung on the walls, next to a big poster of his favorite Wide Receiver, and a potted fern rested in the corner nearest the door. Ronald did not want to think about the trouble Johnny had to have gone through to get approval to keep that plant in his office, let alone to keep it alive all this time.

Johnny plopped down into his chair, a simple wooden office chair on a swivel, and gestured for Ronald and Kathleen to do the same; two plain wooden chairs sat along the wall opposite the door, and caddy-corner to the file cabinets. Ronald grinned in thanks and settled down. Kathleen took a moment to close the door, earning the smallest of quirked eyebrows from Johnny, before joining him.

"What do you need, Ron?" Johnny was alway straight and to the point.

Ronald drew in a deep breath, held it for a second. This was a stretch, even considering the history he shared with Johnny. For a moment he considered forgetting the entire thing, smiling and making a joke out of it. He could certainly get a laugh out of his old friend, deflect from what was really going on… No, they needed answers. Reluctantly, Ronald push ahead.

"We need to identify some people from their photographs," he began.

Johnny looked at him askance. "That's not so hard."

"They're dead, Johnny."

The policeman's face instantly became a mask of seriousness, his tone one of pure business. "What are you talking about?"

With a sigh, Ronald related the story of Samuelson and their trip to the house, their findings in the cellar, and their suspicions. When he was through, Johnny let out a long breath.

"Jesus, Ron." He looked away, toward one of his award citations, for a long moment before speaking again. "Look, buddy. I think you really need to leave this one alone. Let the guys up-County deal with it, and coordinate with Homicide here. They'll find this Samuelson guy, or whoever he is. No one will really think you were involved." He smiled. It was certainly intended to be a comforting smile, but it fell well short.

Ronald shook his head. "This guy decided to screw with us for a reason, Johnny. I…we…need to find out why."

Johnny frowned, but did not reply.

"Ah hell, Johnny. You know how often your boys in the force fuck things up. You've seen it. Help me out here."

Johnny's frown only grew deeper. For a few seconds there, Ronald actually thought Johnny might slap the cuffs on him and Kathleen both. Then, after what seemed an eternity, he nodded and exhaled loudly, his cheeks puffing outwards as he blew. "You got the pictures?"

Ronald gestured toward Kathleen, who opened up the small briefcase she was carrying and withdrew the prints. She handed them over and Johnny leafed through. He turned a barely-perceptible shade paler than normal as he beheld the images.

"Jesus," Johnny breathed.

"Exactly. Think your facial recognition programs can get anything off of them?"

Johnny shrugged. "Ought to." He paused, scratching at his ear for a moment. "You know the up-County homicide guys will probably send these down, if they haven't already, and our boys will run them first thing. I could just get you copies."

"No." Kathleen was supposed to keep quiet and let Ronald do the talking. Big surprise she did not last very long in that job. Not that Ronald could blame her, necessarily. He agreed with her sentiment about not waiting.

Johnny looked between the two of them. Kathleen's jaw was set, and Ronald supposed he probably looked just as immovable as she. Finally, Johnny nodded. "Alright. I'll see what I can do. I'll call you tomorrow."

"Thanks pal." Ronald shook his hand and as always had to hold back wincing a bit at the other man's grip.

THE CALL DID NOT COME the next day, but rather two days later, at 10:30. And it was not from Johnny.

Ronald picked up the phone and recited the standard Davidson & Harper phone greeting - had to at least sound professional - and immediately wished he had not.

"Get your ass in here, Harper!" came the gruff, angry-sounding voice he knew so well. Captain Bixbie.

Ronald groaned inwardly. "Good morning, Captain," he replied with as much cheeriness as he could muster.

It didn't help.

"There will be a car out front your office in five minutes. You, and that partner of yours, will not give the officers any trouble. You're just going to get in the car with them. Understood?"

Ronald glanced over at Kathleen, who was watching from her desk, one eyebrow quirked upward curiously. He gave a little shrug and a thumbs down, and her face grew grim.

"Ok, five minutes. Looking forward to it."

Bixbie just grunted, and the line went dead.

"That what I think it was," Kathleen asked.

Ronald nodded.

"Crap."

He agreed completely.

Captain Bixbie was everything the stereotypical Police Captain was not: lean, tall, with youthful features that did not match his age, yellow-brown hair without a trace of grey that hung to his shoulders. He was impeccably dressed in a suit that had to be taylor made, it fit him so well. His office was neat and organized, everything arranged just-so. Even the bulletin board on his wall, normally cluttered with wanted posters, announcements, or whatever, was almost severe in its lines and columns of papers. And there was not even a hint of cigarette odor in the place. Unnatural.

Ronald and Kathleen sat in padded chairs—the padding was actually halfway comfortable—across from Bixbie's cider block-shaped desk, awaiting the Captain's ire. Johnny stood at parade rest along the wall next to the bulletin board. He did not look happy.

Ronald couldn't blame him. Bixbie was legendary for his outbursts.

"Davidson and Harper," Bixbie said, his voice gravelly and disapproving. "You two have been a royal pain in my ass, you know that?"

Ronald could not help smiling. It was good to hear all his

efforts had not been vain. Beside him, Kathleen shifted in her seat but kept her face smooth.

Bixbie continued, "I don't appreciate your meddling, but," His mouth twisted into something that might have been a smile, except it looked more like a sneer, "when Lieutenant Tennebaum showed me what you found… Well, I think we can let it slide this time." Why that little… Ronald had not thought Johnny would rat them out. Get caught, maybe, but not sell them out.

Wait. What did Bixbie just say?

Bixbie picked up a small remote control that lay on his desk and clicked it. A flat screen that hung on the wall to Ron's left flickered to life, and Bixbie nodded at Johnny.

Johnny came to attention, then nodded in return and turned his attention to Ronald and Kathleen. He did not even have the grace to look apologetic. "I ran the pictures you gave me through facial recognition. It took a while, but we found several matches."

He walked over to the Captain and took the remote, then clicked the button again. On the flat screen, the pictures of three women appeared. All were in their mid-30s, white, and blonde. They were best described as plain: not ugly, but not beautiful either. A few pounds overweight. And, Ronald surmised from the shape of their mouths, happy.

"These woman all disappeared in the last two years," Johnny said. "Mary Gibbons was last seen two counties over, walking her dog on a Sunday morning. Lisa Carpenter vanished from her home in Springfield last October. Her boyfriend was supposed to come over for dinner, but when he showed up, she was not there." He clicked the remote again and the first two pictures faded, leaving the last woman's image to fill the screen. "And then we have Melanie Fisher."

Johnny looked back at Captain Bixbie, who nodded before taking over the floor again. "Mrs. Fisher was reported missing by her husband, Jeremy, six months ago. You may recall the case from the news reporting."

Ronald frowned. It did not ring a bell, per say. But then, he had been rather busy when all this happened. Recovering from a gunshot wound will do that to you.

Kathleen piped up, "I remember that." She looked at the screen for a long moment, frowning. "But I thought that case was solved. Didn't they arrest her husband, or something?"

Silence was Bixbie's only reply for several seconds. He did *not* look pleased at all.

"That's where things become interesting. Her husband was a taken into custody as a person of interest, but released after questioning." He gestured to Johnny, who clicked the remote again, and a new image appeared on the screen. "Recognize him?"

Ronald did indeed recognize the man in the picture - Samuelson.

"Son of a bitch," he said. In unison with Kathleen, who looked as stunned - as *pissed* - as he felt.

"Thought that would get your attention," Bixbie said in a wry tone. "A week after he was released, the cops up-County discovered evidence that linked all three disappearances and pointed to Fisher as the culprit behind all of them. But when they went to arrest him, he had vanished."

"You've got to be kidding me," Ronald said. "Why would he suddenly come out of hiding if he was the bad guy?"

Johnny spoke up. "That is why I brought the Captain into this, Ron. If you look a bit deeper into this case..." He shook his head, frowning. "Have you ever heard the term, orgy of evidence?"

"Sure. That's when you find all the evidence to solve the case in one fell swoop. It's quite convenient."

Kathleen snorted. "It also never really happens that way in real life."

"Exactly. But it seems that's what happened here. The homicide guys up-county all of a sudden went from nothing, only suspicion, to fingerprints, DNA evidence, hell even photographs." Johnny hit the remote again and another set of images filled the screen: tagged evidence, pdfs of coroner's reports, and photographs showing all three women in various locations - both dead and alive.

"So you're saying, what, that he was set up?"

Bixbie nodded, leaning forward in his desk. "Precisely, Miss Davidson. We did a little digging yesterday, after LT Tennebaum showed me what he found. Take a look at these pictures."

Johnny actuated the remote, and the three pictures showing the women alive expanded from the collage to fill the entire screen. All showed the women, smiling, in a park setting. Two were alone, one with a group of friends, and all appeared to be having a good time. All the same, there was something...

"Is that the same park?" As soon as Kathleen voiced the thought, Ronald realized she was correct. The three missing—dead—women had all visited the same park.

"It is," Johnny said. "And what's more, from the time stamps in the photos' metadata, they were all there on the same day."

Well, that was something. "Ok," Ronald said. "So now we know when the killer picked them out."

"We know more than that." Johnny tapped the remote again and the image of Mrs. Fisher expanded to take up the entire screen. She was sitting on the side of a small fountain that was carved in the shape of a cherub sitting atop a fish that was spitting water. Ronald's parents had a similar fountain in their yard when he was growing up; there was nothing special about it. What was he supposed to...

He saw it. Over Mrs. Fisher's shoulder, a couple was sitting on a bench on the far side of the fountain. Or at least the woman was sitting. The man was down on his knees as though proposing. There was something familiar about the man.

"Who is that?" he asked, standing up and walking to the screen. He pointed at the couple.

He could almost hear the satisfied grin on Johnny's face as he replied, "You're going to love this."

The picture zoomed in, and was reduced to pixels for a moment as the display processor adjusted. Then it cleared and the man's features became more clear. He was instantly recognizable now.

"Holy shee-it," Ronald breathed. "Is that Detective Barnes?"

"So what?" Kathleen sniffed and waved a dismissive hand. "So he happened to be in that park with his fiancé on that day. You may not like him but his presence means nothing."

"Except that's not his fiancé," Bixbie said. "She said no."

Ronald's eyebrows climbed on his head and he burst out laughing. Oh that was just awesome. "She has good judgment."

"She's also dead."

Ronald had to do a double-take on that. Was Bixbie serious? The Captain's severe expression said he was. Holy shit.

"What happened to her?" Kathleen asked.

Bixbie scowled. "After the break-up, she apparently decided to move back home to Connecticut. She had a blowout on the interstate. Flipped her car over the embankment and into the path of a sixteen-wheeler heading the other way."

Ronald winced. That was a bad way to go. Not the worst ever, but still bad. All the same, accidents happen. It sucked, and it was a horrible coincidence, but this accident did not mean anything for the case. He opened his mouth to say as much, but Johnny cut him off.

"Not at all connected, right?" One of his eyebrows quirked upward. "That's what we thought too. At first." He clicked the remote, and the images of the three murdered women came back up on the screen, along with a fourth. She could have been a sister to any of the three, she looked so similar to them. "This is Barnes' ex. Quite a resemblance, eh?"

"That does not mean anything either. There are lots of blonde women out there," Kathleen said, running her hand meaningfully through her own locks.

Bixbie nodded in agreement. "True. But just to be safe we checked out the good Detective's background. Turns out he used to own the house Fisher sent you to up-County. Lived in it with his almost-fiancé. He sold it a bit more than two years ago, after she passed away, to his cousin. Or so the county recorder's office said. But couldn't find any financial records that would correspond to a real estate sale, and his cousin has not been in the state since she joined the Air Force five years ago."

"Something smells fishy," Ronald said, earning nods of agreement from both cops.

Kathleen frowned, looking at the screen through narrowed eyes. "So you're saying Detective Barnes killed all these women and then tried to pin it on Fisher." She turned her gaze on Bixbie and Johnny in turn. "That *is* what you're saying?"

Bixbie and Johnny eyed each other for a long moment. Finally, Bixbie shrugged slightly and looked back at Ronald and Kathleen. His expression gave nothing away, but Ronald thought he detected a flash of something—rage? Indignation? —in his eyes.

"That is our theory," Bixbie said, his tone icy. "The women all bore a striking resemblance to the one who jilted him. He never got the chance to get even with her, so..." Bixbie spread his hands, his lips twisting into a sneer of distaste. "It's a little thin, but it was enough to convince Judge Hooper to grant us search warrants. We sent a team up-County to coordinate with the local authorities and investigate further. We should know more in a few days, tops." He took a deep breath, then managed a small smile. "But I wanted you to know that you had not been put through all that trouble for nothing."

Ronald swallowed, unsure how to respond. "Thanks. I guess." He glanced at Kathleen, who looked similarly poleaxed. It was not often the cops were courteous, let alone collegial, toward them. Maybe this was the start of a new, better working relationship.

Bixbie stood then and stepped around his desk. "Don't thank me. You're still a pain in my ass." He crossed his arms over his chest. He was not a particularly large man, but Ronald found himself looking at his eyes as though from a platform far beneath him, he was that good at looming. "I could lock both of you up for interfering in Police business. You know that, right?" Ronald did not trust himself to answer; the snark rose unbidden to the surface, and he was sure it would not serve them well to give voice to it. Bixbie continued, "Next time, someone comes to you with information concerning a possible crime, you bring it to us. Immediately. No delays. No investigation beforehand. *Right the hell now!*" His eyes narrowed and he looked first at Ronald then Kathleen with a gaze that would to Medusa to stone. "We clear?"

So much for collegial.

THREE WEEKS LATER, the news broke. And boy, did it break. It's not every day a policeman actually gets publicly disciplined; they most of the time closed their ranks, from what Ronald had seen. Which is why he never joined the force after the Corps. Oh, he had offers aplenty, but the power without accountability was not something he was comfortable with. And besides, it did not make sense to leave one government structured pay chart just to jump into a second one. He figured there was greater earning potential out in the real world.

Or at least, that's what he told himself.

Regardless, this was not just some public chastisement. cops almost never made the perp walk, so the media had a field day when Barnes walked his. And for a trio of homicides, no less! The reporters were going to dine out on this story for months.

Ronald clicked off the small television that sat atop one of the file cabinets in his office and leaned back in his chair, satisfied. "Not too shabby, huh?"

Kathleen hardly looked up from the paperwork she was filling out. "Don't throw your arm out of its socket patting yourself on the back. We didn't really do anything on this one."

Ronald sniffed. "Just shed light on a set of cases that was going the wrong way. Helped clear an innocent man, brought a killer to justice." He pushed the chair back and stood. "Shoot, I feel positively heroic."

Kathleen just chuckled, shaking her head slowly.

She was right, of course. All the same, it felt good to see things come to a fitting end. Ronald hoped Fisher, wherever he was, was watching that news feed. Finally he could restart his life without looking over his shoulder. That was worth a lot. And a good thing to, considering he still had a bill to pay, to cover their time and expenses.

Ron doubted they would ever see a penny of that money. Oh well.

He strode over to the coat rack near the door and donned his leather jacket, taking a moment to look around the small office. Yep, much better than being a cop.

"See you tomorrow," he said.

Kathleen grunted out a goodbye and he stepped out of the office. As the door swung shut behind him, Ronald thought he heard her laughing to herself.

Beach Bags

A Short Beach Mystery

Michael Kingswood

Beach Bags

An abandoned bag, filled with money and with what appears to be a bloody handprint on the side, upends Harry's relaxing day at the beach.

A light-brown leather handbag doesn't normally just hang out on the beach by itself, but for some reason this one was. No one's blanket or umbrella lay within a hundred feet of it. In fact, except for the little indentation the bag left, the sand appeared to have not been disturbed at all for almost that same area around it.

Harry had just decided he had enough of sweltering on the sand for one day, and that it was time for a cool swim. He packed, donned his navy blue Ron Jon tank top, folded up his beach chair, and was tramping back toward the narrow path that cut through the dunes to the street his vacation rental lay on when he spied it. Normally he wouldn't really have cared to notice, but the strangeness of a bag like that, more a valise than the sort of bag a person would bring to the beach, drew his eye. He slowed and came to a stop, squinting at it from behind the dark lenses of his shades, and frowned.

He turned to the closest people to him, a plump and sunburning couple in their mid-50s who clearly were from somewhere north, and cooler, and raised his voice to carry to them. "Hey, you know whose bag that is?"

The woman, in a one-piece multicolored swimsuit, raised her head from where she had been dozing in her reclining chair, looked toward the bag Harry was pointing at, and shrugged. "Haven't seen anyone near it all morning."

"Was it there when you got here?"

The woman traded looks with her husband, but also shrugged. "Not sure." She paused, looking back at Harry for a second as though waiting for another question. When he didn't immediately follow up, she sank back into her chair and let her head loll back comfortably again.

Harry rolled his eyes. Tourists.

Frowning, he turned back to the bag and pondered it for a few seconds. It really was none of his business. Hell, the owner would probably be back for it any minute now. And the pool was calling out sweetly to him. That, and a cold beer. He almost turned away, but then he noticed something else - a darker patch on the side of the bag, reddish, and shaped like…

It was a handprint. What the hell?

Harry dropped his beach bag and the folding chair, then hurried over to where the bag lay in the sand. He squatted down and looked more closely at it, and at the handprint. It was definitely reddish, and glistened slightly in the light of the noonday sun. Suddenly, he no longer felt the heat of the muggy July day; the chill going up his spine more than washed it away.

Licking his lips with a tongue that had suddenly gone dry, he reached out one finger and touched the handprint. It was wet, sticky, and the fingertip came away red.

He should have run away right then. Run away and called the cops. Because seriously, a bag with a bloody handprint lying on the beach? Not only was it bad news, it was cliched bad news. But for whatever reason he could not stop himself from instead grasping the brass-colored handle on the zipper that closed the bag's main compartment and pulling it open.

The sun illuminated the contents easily, and the breath caught in Harry's throat.

That was a lot of money. It was loose, unbundled, but it looked like mostly 20s and 50s, and it filled the bag most of the way.

What was going on here?

"Hi neighbor!"

Harry jerked upright at the sound of a young female voice, and turned. She stood about five foot five, and had wavy dark-brown hair that hung to just past her shoulders, though this morning it was pulled back into a ponytail. Her bikini was pink with little white flower shapes on it, and she filled it out nicely: the muscles of her abdomen were just barely visible, she had nice hips, and Harry's trained eye placed her in a B-cup, maybe a small C. She had shades on, and had a floral-pattern beach bag thrown over one shoulder. A pair of black-soled flip flops dangled from her left hand.

He recognized her immediately. Stacey, from the rental next door to his. He'd noticed her when she and her friends moved in and they had exchanged hellos, but that was it, though he had made a mental note to follow up with her at the first opportunity.

Stacey grinned at him, a warm and inviting grin that Harry was tempted to imagine was just for him. Of course, he knew better. "Harry, right?"

He wiped his hands off on his swim trunks and straightened fully. "Yeah. Good to see you again, Stacey." He looked quickly around and, seeing she was alone, added, "Your girlfriends aren't joining you today?"

She shrugged. "They wanted to go shopping."

Harry blinked. "But you didn't?"

"Nope."

A woman who didn't want to go shopping? Harry definitely needed to follow up with her. All of a sudden he was thinking maybe the swim could wait. Maybe he ought to stay on the beach for a while. Or even better, maybe she'd care for a dip is a fresh water pool instead of the salty sea. As soon as he figured out what to do about -

"That's Karen's bag," Stacey said, out of the blue, and Harry blinked in surprise.

"Who's Karen?"

"She's renting the house next to us, on the other side from you." Stacey looked around, frowning. "Where is she?"

Well, that was one mystery solved. Harry glanced over toward the dunes. His house was to the left after the path met up with the road. Stacey and her friends' was directly adjacent to the path on the right. Which meant Karen's was the next one on the right, and just about even with where the bag was lying. Someone could have thrown the bag over the dune. But why get rid of a bag full of money?

Given the bloody handprint, he didn't have a lot of trouble coming up with all sorts of reasons why, come to think on it.

"Um, Stacey," Harry said, "I think she might be in trouble. I just found this here, and, well, look for yourself." He squatted down again and gestured toward the bag.

Stacey, frowning, stepped closer and leaned over to examine the bag more closely. As she did, the sun struck her shades at just the right angle to allow him to see her eyes go wide. Her jaw dropped open. "Is that - ?"

Harry nodded. "I think so." He looked closely at her. "What do you know about Karen?"

Stacey gave a little shake and, pursing her lips, straightened. "Not much. She's an artist, I think. Lives there with her daughter."

"No husband?"

She shook her head. "I don't think so." She cocked her head to the side, looking at him with an odd expression on her face. "Are you a cop or something?"

He snorted and stood back up. "No. Not anymore."

Her eyebrow lifted, and he saw the question there. But she didn't ask it, instead saying, "But you've called them, right?"

"No, like I said I just found the bag." Although, come to think on it… "You said she's an artist. Does she paint?"

"I dunno, I guess. Why - ?" Then she burst out in a little, relieved, laugh. "That could be paint. Red paint!"

Well, blood was not nearly as thick as paint, so Harry sort of doubted it. Maybe watercolor? Still, if it helped Stacey keep calm while they figured this out…and who knows, it could be true. "Could be. I hope so." He bent over and picked up the bag by its carrying handles. "Before we get the cops involved, let's make sure this isn't just us jumping to conclusions." He looked back at Stacey. "Will you come along? You've met her.

Might be weird if a stranger showed up with her her bag of money."

She chuckled and nodded briskly. "No kidding."

Harry took a minute to pick up his things and get all of his burdens more comfortably arranged. Then the two of them turned toward the path leading through the dunes.

As they came out the other side, he nodded toward his place, on the left. "I'm going to drop my stuff off real quick," he said, and she nodded concurrence.

His rental had a grey stone privacy wall between the path and his back yard, just high enough that he could peek over it on tip-toe. It was broken halfway between its commencement just below the dune and the street ahead by a red-stained wooden gate with a simple lifting latch. Not exactly prime security, but it did the job of keeping prying eyes out.

Opening the gate, he flashed Stacey a quick grin then stepped onto his pool deck.

Poured cement, with blue and white fish-shapes inlaid around the perimeter of the pool, the deck area was simple enough to almost be elegant. A trio of yellow and white chaise lounges sat on the dune side of the pool, and a glass-topped table with seating for six and a matching yellow and white umbrella sat off to the right on the house side, near a bricked-in barbecue pit and a granite-topped bar complete with kegorator.

Not a bad place to hang out.

As Harry dropped his bag and chair, leaning the later against the bar, Stacey let out a low whistle.

"Nice pool," she said, appreciatively. "Sure beats what we've got at our place."

Harry shrugged. "It works." He turned back to her and hefted the bag of money. "You ready?"

She looked away from the inviting water toward the bag,

and Harry could see the concern in her expression. She nodded.

Stacey led the way back out the gate.

Karen's house was a one-story beige-stucco bungalow set back from the road about thirty feet. In lieu of a driveway, the area immediately off the road was just graveled in, offering space to park three cars. Maybe four, if they squeezed. Right now there were two: a red Honda Civic and a silvery-grey Subaru Outback. A pair of palm trees stood on either side of a little walking path leading from the parking area to her white-painted front door. Long windows on either side of the door offered views into the living areas, but the interior was dark compared with the noonday sun and Harry could not see much detail.

He frowned, considering the cars for a second. "Either of those hers?"

Stacey nodded. "The Outback." She paused, the added, "Don't know about the other one."

Well, Karen was home at least. That was something, and helped rule out foul play. At least, that's what Harry hoped.

They walked up to the front door, and Harry knocked three times. When, after a long ten count, no one came to the door, he looked over at Stacey, who gave a little shrug.

"She's here," she said, and reached out and tried the doorknob.

It turned freely, and the door swung open on silent hinges.

The lights were out in the entryway and the living room beyond, but there was more than enough sunlight to see details. The floor was yellow-brown stone, polished to a dull shine. The furnishings in the living room were spare, no frills. Which probably meant they were pretty darn comfortable. A small wood stove stood in the rear left corner, the black cast iron of its chimney rising through the ceiling in place of a fire-place. Directly opposite the front door, an open archway led to a hallway leading further back into the house. On the rear wall was a large oil painting of the seashore. Windows dominated the left-hand wall, and the wall to the right held framed pictures of a homely blonde woman of about thirty-five with a pre-teen girl who had her same hair, nose, and eyes.

"Karen and daughter, I presume," Harry said to himself. He had not intended the words for Stacey, but she responded with a "Yeah" anyway.

They hesitated in the doorway, watching and listening. The place seemed deserted; there was no sound besides their breathing. If not for the lingering odor of bacon on the air, Harry would have thought no one had been in the house in days.

"Doesn't look like she's here," he said, doubtfully.

Stacey looked left and right again, then took a slow step inside, pushing her shades up onto her forehead. "Karen?" she called. "Are you home?"

A muffled noise, hard to put a name on, came from the back of the house. There was someone here after all.

Harry traded a glance with Stacey then, handing the bag of money to her, took the lead into the hallway. It wasn't exactly narrow, but he would have to turn sideways to let another person pass comfortably down it. More photos of family and friends hung on the walls, and they passed a powder room on the right, then a small bedroom that had been turned into an office on the left. Then the hallway opened into a combination kitchen/dining area that looked like it had been transported from the 60s.

It was all linoleum and garish colors, with old appliances and a dining room table that appeared to have been painted and re-painted several times from all the streaks of color on it. Off to the right, past the kitchen area, another hallway led, presumably, to the bedrooms, and there was a sliding glass door at the rear leading out into the back yard. Royal blue hanging drapes hanging from casters in the ceiling were mostly drawn across the rear door and the floor-to-ceiling window that took up most of the rest of the back wall, letting sunlight spill into the room.

The sliding glass door was open, and the sea breeze made the drapes billow slightly as it brought the day's heat inside to fight with the air conditioned air within.

As he stepped into the room, it was obvious to Harry that there had been some kind of trouble here. Dining chairs were knocked over, and an empty glass lay on the floor next to one of them, a spreading puddle of water marking its former contents. Two plates, both with bacon and eggs lying half-eaten on them, sat on the table, and dirty pans were on the stove.

"This doesn't look good," Stacey said as she looked around. Then, more loudly, she called out, "Karen!" She waited a second, then turned to look at Harry. "I think we should call the cops now."

Harry was just nodding his head to agree when another noise came from the back yard. It sounded like an impact of some sort, and maybe a voice, but he couldn't make out the words. But the tone was unmistakable: anger, desperation, and malice all rolled into one.

"Make the call," he said, and hurried to the sliding glass door.

The back yard was nothing fancy. A smallish concrete pad where Karen had set up a grill and a little metal-and-plastic table set for two, and the rest was grass going to sand as it approached the dunes in the rear. About halfway back lay a new-looking wooden outbuilding. More than a shed, it was almost the size of the kitchen/dining room in the house, painted grey, and had electrical wires running to it from the corner of the house. It had a set of double doors for an entrance that were closed, but a quick glance around showed nowhere else anyone could be on the property, and privacy fences on either side would have prevented them from going into the neighbors' places.

So the out-building it was.

Harry strode over with the quick, purposeful walk he reserved for when he really meant business…and he thought someone might be watching. Over the years, that walk alone had prompted some tough guys to back down from a fight. Here's hoping a similar result happened this time.

Reaching the double doors, he paused. From inside the out-building he could hear sounds of movement, or things being pushed or thrown around. And something else, almost like a voice but muffled. Then something shattered within and he heard a loud, salty curse.

"Where is it?"

That was the first intelligible words he had heard. They came from a female voice, filled with anger. And near-panic. Whoever that was, she was on the ragged edge. Probably knew she was jail-bound but was past the line with no way to pull back. That kind of person was dangerous.

Time to put a stop to whatever was going on in there. He grasped the doorknobs and pulled the double-doors open.

The inside of the out-building was set up as a studio. Easels and canvases were stacked against the left wall, the ones near the back blank and the ones toward the front splashed with swaths of color of all shades in random patterns, or filled with paintings of people in various poses, and a few landscapes as well. To Harry's untrained eye, the paintings didn't look like anything special.

The right-hand side of the building held pottery and sculpting equipment. There was a potter's wheel and a kiln, an unstained wooden chest of drawers that was topped with a bunch of jars and containers, and resting on a little stand toward the rear a block of what looked like marble, but probably wasn't, that someone had begun carving into. The vague form of a four-legged animal was beginning to take shape, but it was far from done.

The entire place was lit by a pair of fluorescent tracks mounted to the ceiling, and a little wall-mounted air conditioning unit whirred in the back corner.

Harry took all that in at a glance, but what caught and held his attention like a vice was the action in the center of the building. The blonde woman and girl from the picture in the living room of the house were tied hand and foot, gagged, and plopped down next to next other on a threadbare love seat that sat against the middle of the rear wall. Both were in their pajamas, and looked frightened out of their wits. A short, stocky, black-haired fellow in blue jeans and a loose short-sleeved white collared shirt, with sweat stains running down the back from the day's heat, stood looming over them.

A woman, chubby with close-cropped hair that had been died pink and a loop-earring through her left nostril, was rummaging through the chest of drawers. She wore a loose-fitting navy blue blouse that was unbuttoned one button too far and slightly too tight white pants, and her face was a mask of chagrin.

Both of the bad guys spun to face him as he opened the doors, the influx of sunlight giving his presence away immediately. Both jaws dropped in surprise, and both sets of eyes widened in chagrin.

"Well, isn't this special?" Harry said before they could get a word out, and he crossed his arms over his chest. He was painfully aware that he likely appeared less than threatening in his board shorts, tank top, and flip flops, with his shades pushed up onto his forehead. More like a surfer than a savior. But he had a couple inches on the guy, and was in better shape besides. Hopefully these two would be spooked enough about what they were doing to not start anything.

"You guys are in heaps of trouble, you know that?" he continued, keeping his tone as conversational as possible. "The police are on the way, so how about you make nice, untie the lady and her daughter, sit down over there," he jerked his jaw toward a space on the floor between the kiln and the partially completed sculpture, "and be a good little boy and girl until they get here. No need to make this harder than it's going to be."

The woman and the man traded looks. She scowled and jerked her head Harry's way.

Let's you and him fight. Typical. Even odds she had made him do the tying up, too.

The guy didn't look enthused, but he squared his shoulders and took a step in Harry's direction. "You made a big mistake coming here, buddy," he said in a tone that almost but not quite didn't proclaim confidence that he was going to put Harry down.

"That makes three of us then," Harry said, not moving but putting on what he hoped was a cheerful smile. "Don't make another one."

The guy sniffed and came forward, driving an obvious, slow, and lumbering right fist toward Harry's face.

Harry managed to sigh with disgust as he bobbed to the side out of the punch's way and drove a left upper cut into the guy's liver.

The guy's eyes bugged out and he coughed out an "Ugh!" as he doubled over.

Harry shook his head and considered for a second, the popped him in the side of the jaw with a right. The guy went down onto his left side and stayed there, groaning.

"Moron." Harry looked up from the vanquished man toward Pink-hair. He pointed a commanding finger at her, then at the floor. "Siddown."

Pink-hair's eyes had gone wide as saucers. They were fixed

on her fallen white knight, and she was shaking hard. Either she hadn't heard Harry or his words hadn't registered.

He tried again. "Sit. Down. Now," he said again, putting a biting command into each word.

She sat.

Behind him, he heard footsteps through grass, then Stacey's voice. "Nice work," she said as he came up next to him. She eyed the fallen man appreciatively, then turned to grin at Harry after a second. It was the kind of look that would have sent butterflies through his belly back when he was thirteen. Today they made him grin inwardly, in anticipation.

"Why don't you untie them? I'll watch these two."

Stacey bobbed a nod, then set to it.

The police arrived fifteen minutes later, and they set to the taking of statements and booking the bad guys.

Turns out Pink-hair was Karen's manager. Agent. Whatever they called it. She had been hounding Karen for weeks, claiming Karen owed her money for an exhibition she had booked a month ago, which of course Karen denied. When Karen showed up with Chad—of course they White Knight's name was Chad—demanding the money, Karen had sent her daughter to hide the bag while she dealt with them. The daughter had heard the growing altercation and panicked, knocking over a can of red paint in her haste to find a hiding spot. In the end she had thrown the bag up onto the dune, and then ran back to try to help. She had thrown the bag harder than she thought, because it made it over the dune entirely.

Chad was good at forcing women into submission, if nothing else. He had tied and gagged them while Pink-hair searched around, and that's when Harry walked in.

It didn't seem like they had much of a plan beyond that. But then, those types never did, did they? Even money Pink Hair had a legit complaint. Harry wouldn't have been surprised to learn Karen had been stiffing her for a long time. Not that it mattered now. Morons.

Two hours later, the cops were gone with the perps, and Karen and her daughter had followed in their own car to finish giving their statements at the station.

Harry and Stacey watched the little caravan pull off down the road from the front of Karen's house, and Harry couldn't help but feel quite satisfied with himself. He'd saved the day and it wasn't even three o'clock. Not a bad bit of work, if he did say so himself.

"All's well that ends well, eh?" He turned to look fully at Stacey, and put on his best, most inviting smile. "I don't know about you, but I think this calls for a celebration."

She returned his look gamely, arching one eyebrow. "Oh yeah?" She moved a couple inches closer, looking up at his face with the smallest of secretive smiles. "What did you have in mind?"

"I was thinking of grilling up a burger, having a beer, and taking a dip in the pool." He let that sink in for a second. "You game?"

That little smile grew to a warm, almost sultry grin. "Sounds good."

Yeah, a pretty good day's work. And it was looking like the rest of the day was going to be even better.

Message From The Author

Thank you for reading my book. I hope you enjoyed reading it as much as I enjoyed writing it.

Every review helps an author out, so whether you loved this book, hated it, or something in between, please take a minute to tell other readers what you thought. All of the online retailers make it very easy to do, and I would really appreciate it.

Feel free to come say hi at my website or on Facebook. I always enjoy hearing from readers, especially since you all are, collectively, my boss.

I also have a weekly podcast, Story Time With Michael Kingswood, where I read stories and talk through some of the latest goings on in my world. I'd love to see you there.

Thanks again. My best to you and yours.

Warm Regards,
Michael Kingswood

Mailing List

If you enjoyed this book and would like word on new releases and special deals from Michael Kingswood, sign up for his newsletter on his website. Guaranteed to be spam-free, you can opt out at any time. And you can rest assured he will not share your information with anyone, for any reason.

https://michaelkingswood.com/newsletter-signup/

About The Author

Michael Kingswood is 20-year veteran of the US Navy submarine force and a lifelong fan of science fiction and fantasy literature. His work has appeared in numerous collections and anthologies, to include the Fiction River Anthology series from WMG publishing. He holds a bachelors degree in Mechanical Engineering as well as a Master of Engineering Management and a Master of Business Administration. He has four children and currently resides in San Diego.

Find Michael Kingswood online at:

www.michaelkingswood.com

www.facebook.com/michael.kingswood

steemit.com/@michaelkingswood

Novellas

What Lurks Between

The Necromancer's Lair

The Champion

Veritas Morte

Story Collections

Tales Of Adventure #1

Tales Of Adventure #2

Short Story 10-Pack

A Jar Of Mixed Treats

Short Mystery 10-Pack

Short Fiction

Michael has also published a number of shorter works, links to which can be found on his website.